THE SEVEN SISTERS

SELECTED CHINESE FOLK STORIES

Fredonia Books
Amsterdam, The Netherlands

The Seven Sisters:
Selected Chinese Folk Stories

Compiled and Edited by
David Falkayn

ISBN: 1-4101-0250-5

Reprinted from the 1965 edition

Fredonia Books
Amsterdam, The Netherlands
http://www.fredoniabooks.com

Contents

Contents

Date-Stone

(A Han Story)

Once upon a time, in a village at the foot of a mountain there lived a man and his wife. They longed for a child, and used to say: "How happy we should be if we only had a child, even if he were as tiny as a date-stone." Not long afterwards, so the story says, the wife gave birth to a son, who was really no bigger than a date-stone. Otherwise, there would be no story. The couple were very happy and named him Date-Stone.

One year, two years, and a few more years passed but the child had not grown a bit. One day the father said: "Date-Stone! I've been happy without reason. What is the good of trying to raise a child like you?" His mother also said: "My dear, you haven't grown, not even a little bit. I'm worried about you too!" Date-Stone answered: "There's no need to worry, Father and Mother. Don't judge me by my size. I'll do as much as anyone else."

Date-Stone was very painstaking and worked every day. His small body was very strong and healthy and he learned to do many kinds of jobs. He knew how to drive a donkey and to plough. He would collect more firewood than anyone else, because he was able to leap as high as the roof and climb to heights which frightened others. The neighbours all praised him and often scolded their own children, saying: "Small as Date-Stone is, he works well and none of you are a match for him. Aren't you ashamed?" And so Date-Stone's mother and father began to feel happier.

Date-Stone was not only hard working but also clever. One year there was a severe drought and not a single grain of rice was harvested throughout the whole village. Although there was no food for the villagers the officials from the city came as usual to collect the tax, which was supposed to be paid in kind.

But because the villagers were unable to pay the magistrate gave orders that their oxen and donkeys be confiscated.

Without draft animals it would be impossible for the peasants to till their land the following spring. They were all very worried. But Date-Stone said to them "Don't worry. I have a plan!" Some villagers, who had no faith in him, muttered, "Little people shouldn't talk so big!" But Date-Stone didn't argue with them. He merely replied, "All right. You just wait and see."

That evening Date-Stone ran to the stable kept by the magistrate. With one jump he was over the fence. He then hid himself and waited for the guards to fall asleep. When they were asleep he untied one of the donkeys, and leaping into its ear, he shouted.

The noise awoke the guards and they yelled with fright: "Donkey thief! Donkey thief!" They quickly took up their swords and spears and began to search everywhere. They searched and searched but they couldn't find any thief. But no sooner had they gone back to bed than the shouting was repeated. Again they jumped up, searched around and failed to find the thief. This went on and on until after midnight and the guards were quite exhausted. The captain of the guards said, "Something strange is going on. Don't let's pay any attention to it. Let's go to sleep." They lay down again and being very tired, soon fell into a sound sleep. Then, Date-Stone leaped down from the donkey's ear, opened the door and led every one of the animals back to the village.

The animals had been taken away, but the magistrate wasn't going to give them up that readily. So at daybreak he went with the guards to the village to arrest the peasants. When the villagers were assembled Date-Stone sprang in front of them and said, "I led the animals back. What are you going to do about it?"

The magistrate yelled, "Tie him up! Tie him up!"

The guards then got out some chains and tried to tie Date-Stone up. But he was so small he was able to jump right through the links of the chain and there he stood, laughing at them.

The guards ran round and round in circles, not knowing what to do. But the magistrate was a man of ideas. He said, "Put Date-Stone in a money bag and carry him back to headquarters."

When the magistrate had seated himself comfortably in the hall, he pounded the desk with his fist and shouted: "Thrash him hard!"

Date-Stone leaped here and leaped there, and although the guards tried to thrash him, they couldn't, for he was far too nimble. Burning with rage the magistrate yelled, "Get more guards and more sticks!"

Hearing this order Date-Stone stopped jumping about. With one leap he landed on the magistrate's beard. Then grasping it firmly, he swung to and fro, holding on tightly all the while. Yelling with pain, the magistrate shouted "Knock him off! Knock him off!" The guards rushed in and struck blows that missed Date-Stone but landed on the magistrate,

knocking out all his teeth. Everyone in the hall was frightened and rushed to the aid of the magistrate. Date-Stone strolled merrily away.

Something for Nothing

(A Hui Story)

Twenty years ago, in our village, which was a Moslem one, there lived a wealthy merchant family. They owned many *mou** of land and a large number of pack horses. The head of the family, who was generally known as Old Money Bag, had several wives, but only one of them had borne him a son. Now, as you know, the only son in a rich family is as precious as a gem.

The saying, "like father, like son!" was true in this case. And as the boy grew up, he proved to have the same ways as his father. He spent his days smoking, gambling, feasting and drinking.

Old Money Bag had a caravan of more than a hundred pack animals and he hired more than thirty drivers to take charge of them. After each journey the courtyard was filled with silver, foodstuffs and

---

* A *mou* is equivalent to 0.0666 hectare or 0.1647 acre.

all kinds of goods that they had brought back. The caravan men talked gleefully about the good times they had had in this town or that county. Their descriptions of the delicious fruits alone caused the young son's mouth to water. The caravan always returned with a variety of fruits, but they had lost their freshness on the long journey.

One day Young Money Bag again lost while gambling and when he returned home he had a talk with his father saying, "Father, I want to go out into the world to seek my fortune and enjoy life."

Old Money Bag was very pleased with the boy's decision. "Very well," he said. "If you go on these trips, these filthy drivers will have less chance to swindle us behind our backs. With you with them, they won't dare to cheat me any more." Thoughts about the drivers made him very angry and he cursed them saying, "I've taken care of them all their lives, but they tell people everywhere that I've become wealthy at their expense. Phew! They are all ungrateful dogs!" Regaining his breath he said: "Ahfu, you must learn wisdom, for when I'm gone the family fortune will be in your hands."

When the caravan next returned, Old Money Bag called all his drivers before him and after greeting them he announced: "From now on Ahfu will go with the caravan and all business will be handled by him. Your work will be just to attend to the horses. Ahfu's wishes must be obeyed without question." The drivers uttered not a word.

The next day many horses were loaded with bolts of cloth, women's ornaments, salt and other things for barter and sale. An Iman was asked to come in and read a passage from the scriptures, and the neighbours and relatives were invited to a feast. Then the caravan started out.

For the poor a journey is a miserable experience, but it brings pleasure to the rich. Ahfu was helped on and off his horse and received the best of care wherever he rested for a while or stopped for the night. For him, the trip was complete enjoyment.

Although it was Ahfu's first time away from home, he thought he knew everything·there was to know about trading. To him it was just the same as gambling where it was only necessary to be cunning. If he was clever enough to pick up the right things, he'd certainly get a lot of things for almost nothing and make a big fortune. He believed that any transaction which he handled himself was sure to be conducted with much more skill than by any driver, however experienced.

The caravan proceeded on its way, until one afternoon it arrived at a town. It was small but bustling with activity. After he had settled himself into an inn, Ahfu ordered two of the drivers to accompany him on a tour of the town. They found a Moslem eating-house and had a good meal. Then they went for a stroll to see the sights. They followed a crowd until they came to a street where many people were gathered in front of a small shop. Ahfu, anxious to find out what attracted them, elbowed his way through the crowd and saw a man making delicate marks on paper with a small brush. The man first dabbed the brush in some black ink and then made many small strokes on the paper. Someone in the crowd gave the man a handful of silver coins in exchange for this piece of paper with the delicate markings.

"What is he doing?" Ahfu asked the drivers.

"He is writing! His brush has brought him much fame."

"Can he make a lot of money by doing this?" he inquired.

"Of course he can. With that brush of his, in one day alone he makes a pile of silver."

"Wonderful! What a marvelous way to make so much money. I'll take several dozen of those brushes back with me." After considering the matter carefully Ahfu called one of his drivers and said, "Go and ask him how many brushes he has. I'll buy them all."

The driver did not dare to question his young master's wisdom so he went over to ask about the brushes. At first the calligrapher wasn't willing to sell. But after much persuasion he agreed to part with two of his brushes in exchange for the goods in twenty horse-packs.

That same evening Ahfu gave the writer the goods carried by twenty pack-horses and took the two brushes, putting them into his pocket.

"Ha, ha," laughed Ahfu. "Now money will flow in whenever I wish. And all I gave was twenty horse-packs of goods for these magic brushes." He felt extremely happy.

The caravan proceeded on its way uneventfully until at noon one day it stopped for the midday meal and rest. Not far from the road a peasant was working diligently in his field, undeterred by the weather, regardless of wind or sun.

"What have you got there?" asked Ahfu curiously.

"You mean this thing in my hand? It's a hoe. I depend entirely on this wonderful tool to dig gold and silver, and to feed and clothe myself," replied the peasant.

"Oh, how wonderful. Gold, silver, clothes . . . anything you want. How many of those tools have you got?"

"How many? One is enough to provide for a man for life. Why should I have more than one?"

"This will certainly make me very rich," thought Ahfu. "Sell it to me," he said to the peasant. Then, pointing to the pack-horses beside the road, Ahfu tried to persuade him, "See how many pack-horses

I have. Take the goods from as many of them as you like".

Then the peasant, who only asked for thirty packs, gave Ahfu the hoe in exchange.

"Ha, ha, I can have anything I dream about, and I only traded thirty packs for it!" gloated Ahfu to himself.

He and his men rode on until they came to a big county town. Seeing how busy it was, Ahfu told his drivers that they would stay there for a whole day.

On this occasion, as before, Ahfu took two of the drivers with him to look around. When they arrived at some crossroads they saw a crowd. Ahfu squeezed his way to the centre, where he saw a man showing everyone a small wooden box which he held up so that everyone could see it. "What is he doing?" Ahfu asked the drivers. "He's a conjurer," they replied.

Ahfu watched attentively, as with a few quick movements, the man turned the box around to show his audience that it was empty. Then he covered it with his handkerchief, chanted some strange words and called out: "Come, come, come!" Slowly he removed the handkerchief, and from the same box he took rice, dishes, money, sweets . . . and Goodness knows what else!

Ahfu thought, without doubt this is better than all the other things I've bought. "Hey," he called to the drivers. "Offer him all the rest of our goods for the box."

"Young Master, can't you see it's only a trick?" they asked in amazement.

"Don't dare to question what I do. Just do as I say," scolded Ahfu.

"Ha, ha," he laughed. "Food, wine . . . whenever I want it. And all for only forty packs. I'll make a bigger fortune than my father!"

Now Ahfu had only his horses left. On his return to the inn he thought of a cunning thing to do. So many drivers and horses with nothing for them to carry; to put them up at the inn would cost a great deal of money. The thing to do was to send them home! He distributed the horses among the drivers and told them to return home. Not "daring" to "disobey him", they smiled at each other and departed.

Ahfu thought: "Stupid fools! They'll have to pay out of their own pockets for their horses' keep and their own. Yet they went off so cheerfully! Ha, ha!"

Ahfu laughed happily and thought: "How smoothly the trading went this time! With all these treasures I'll make my fortune."

Ahfu had kept only one horse for himself. After enjoying himself for two more days in the town, on the third morning, he started the return journey happy in the possession of two magic brushes, a magic hoe and a magic box.

Ahfu was a good rider, but he did not like to attend to a horse's needs. He rode hard and unsparingly, until one day the horse dropped dead. Ahfu scrambled to his feet and whipped the poor animal viciously, but it did not move. "If you don't get up I'll leave you!" he threatened. Finally he was forced to continue on foot, carrying the magic things.

Walking was not easy, and at the end of the first day he had only covered a short distance. His feet were blistered and his legs ached. He walked all the next day and spent the last of his money on food and water. The following day, about noon, his feet and legs were hurting him so much that he could go no further. He sat at the side of the road to rest. Then he suddenly thought, the time has come to use my magic things!

First he took out the magic box, turned it around a few times, covered it with his handkerchief and then chanted:

> Magic box, magic box, listen to me,
> Fish and meat, I wish to eat.
> One, two, three!

He slowly removed the handkerchief. Bah! The box was empty! He examined it carefully but it really was empty. Ahfu was now very angry. He raised his whip and slashed at the box until it was smashed to pieces.

"Never mind," he comforted himself. "If one thing fails I still have others. The magic box was a fraud but the hoe is genuine." He picked up the hoe and scratching the ground three times he chanted:

> Magic hoe, magic hoe, listen to me,
> Clothes and hats I do not need,
> What I want is a meal indeed!
> Come, come, come!

He examined the ground carefully but instead of food there was only soil. He tried again but nothing happened. On the ground were several patches of loose earth but not a speck of food. After trying three times Ahfu, now angry, flung the hoe high in the air with all his might, but the weight of the iron blade caused it to turn in the air and the hoe fell right back, hitting him on the head. He howled with pain. He sat rubbing his head with one hand and lashing at the hoe with the other.

After a while Ahfu gave a great yawn, and being a gambler, he thought, never mind, out of three chances I'm sure to win once. I still have the small writing brushes in my pocket. I must hurry to the county town and in one day I'll make more money than I can carry. As he thought of this he struggled to his feet. His legs felt heavy and the soles of his feet burned as if they were being pricked by a hundred pins and needles. But what could he do? There wasn't another soul on the road so there was nothing he could do but walk on. Ahfu yawned repeatedly and cried, "Ai, Mama! Ai, Papa!" Dragging his heavy legs he slowly continued on his weary way.

It was not until the sun had sunk behind the rim of the mountains that he reached a small village. He walked down the street and then sank down on the ground to rest. At last, driven by hunger and thirst he took out his writing brush and began to make marks with it on the ground. It seemed as though he would be luckier with the brush, for in no time his drawing attracted the attention of several women and children. He continued to draw and the crowd grew bigger. Feeling as if he had already gained enough money to load several pack-horses, Ahfu relaxed a little, while happy visions of food and money floated across his mind.

He drew more strokes with the brush and more people gathered but not one gave him any money. Then he called:

> *Magic brush, magic brush!*
> *Make me a pile of money a day.*
> *If anyone wants me to write for him.*
> *Let him hurry up and give me his money.*

But nothing happened. He called again and still there was no money; he shouted the third, fourth and fifth times. Then the spectators began to laugh. After calling the seventh, eighth and ninth time, his throat became dry and still no one brought him any money. He called and called until the sun set and still no one responded.

Darkness slowly fell and the people went home. There were no inns or eating-places in this little village, and Ahfu, who was accustomed only to luxurious food and good living, found that the effort of moaning "Mama" and "Papa" made the hunger pain him even worse. But that was the only thing he was capable of doing, so he went on first moaning and then yelling as if that did any good. . . !

The Story of a Serf

(A Mongolian Story)

Long, long ago on the wide grasslands lived a prince whose lands stretched farther than the eye could see. He was so wealthy and powerful that he had his own army, several hundred serfs and innumerable cattle and sheep. All who lived on the grasslands were in feudal bondage to this cruel prince and completely at his mercy.

Among his many serfs was one by the name of Ulan Bator. This youth was stalwart and skilled in archery. In the air or on the ground nothing escape his arrows and it was well-known that he never missed. Far and near the name of Ulan Bator was renowned.

One day as he was returning from hunting, he met a white-haired old man who said to him: "Ulan Bator, you are now grown up and have reached the age of manhood. As you are a better shot with the bow than anyone else, why haven't you avenged your father's death? Even an eagle that soars high in the blue, leaves his shadow on the ground. Bator! Bator! How can you forget your own father?" Ulan Bator dropped from his saddle, and kneeling before the old man asked, "Who killed my father?" The old man shook his head and answered, "On the 15th there is a full moon. At that time everything will become clear." Then the old man walked away towards the west.

When he had disappeared in the distance Bator mounted his horse and hurried home. He entered the yurt and grasping his mother by the arms he asked, "How did my father die?" His mother was startled at his impetuousness but she soon recovered herself and replied: "I have already told you many times that your father died from a sickness when you were only a year old! Why do you ask again? Who's been talking nonsense to you?" Ulan Bator dared not mention what the old man had told him, but his curiosity was now aroused.

That night Ulan Bator was very restless. Suddenly he heard the sound of muffled crying. He pricked up his ears and listened carefully, and realized that the sound was coming from someone within his own yurt. It must be my mother who is crying, he thought. He arose, tiptoed to his mother's side, and taking her hand in his he knelt beside her, then requestioned, "Mother, why are you crying? Tell me, I'm your son. The loftiest trees may touch the sky but they are very small compared with all the tender care you have shown in bringing me up."

Still crying, his mother finally told him the cause of her grief, "My child, you have now grown into a man and can understand many things. There is something you should know. The only reason that I've kept the truth about your father's death from you, is because I do not want disaster to overtake you too. Your father did not die of a sickness. He was buried alive because he followed Gada who opposed the Prince. As you were only one year old at that time I fled with you in my arms. For eight years I roamed about as a beggar, but the memories of the grasslands and the yurts never faded from my mind, for no one can forget his homeland. After a time I changed my name and came back to the grasslands to become a serf of the Prince once more. I've suffered many abuses and whippings, while patiently waiting for you to grow up. . . ." His mother's voice became choked with sobs. Like beads from a broken string the tears rolled down Bator's face. Then wiping his eyes, he slowly rose to his feet. Clenching his teeth and burning with defiance he snatched his bow from the wall. Then, with his hand on his heart he vowed, "Mother, I will kill the Prince and avenge my father's death!" His mother was alarmed and held him back, saying, "Don't go, my child. You will never succeed." But Bator replied, "Mother, I'm not afraid of him. I'll fight with him to the bitter end." Embracing Bator tightly his mother argued, "My son, listen to your mother . . . you mustn't go. Of course your father's death must be avenged but you cannot do this alone. There's a saying well-known among our old people, 'The best wrestlers can't win if they're outnumbered; the best of horses can't endure a hundred lashes.' Alone, you cannot overcome all the soldiers of the Prince." His mother's warning caused Bator to reconsider his hasty decision.

After that, the songs of Bator were no longer heard across the grasslands. Whenever he left home, his mother was worried and remained within the yurt praying to Buddha. When he returned safely she happily bowed to the image. Yet most of the time she lived in fear. But as sure as the wild geese fly south when the time for migration comes, so all other things happen at their appointed time.

One day the Prince ordered Bator to go hunting with him. Bator's hatred showed in his scornful looks and this angered the Prince. He raised his whip to strike Bator but Bator quickly wrested the whip from him. Then striking him a blow, Bator asked, "Have you forgotten old Ulan, my father. I am going to revenge him!" As he started to strike the Prince for the second time he was overpowered by the guards, tied up and carried off. After a cruel beating he was bound with ropes and thrown into a prison, where he was left alone.

Several days later one of the Prince's henchmen rushed into the prison, untied Bator and dragged him to the tent of the Prince. It was a pitch black night but the Prince's tent was brightly lit. When he saw Bator enter, the Prince, enjoying his power over the helpless prisoner, laughed in a cruel fashion exposing his hideous teeth as he did so. "I have a task for you," he shouted. "A gold ring belonging to the Princess has fallen into the well. Climb down and find it! If you succeed I'll set you free."

Bator burned with fury when he heard this and he replied scornfully, "Everyone knows that your well is bottomless! You talk nonsense when you tell someone to climb inside and find a ring. Why don't you say straight out that you want to kill me. But . . . I'm not afraid. A storm always passes over, the labourers will have their day, and when that time comes I'll break your neck, skin you alive, boil your hide in oil and throw your bones to the dogs. . . ." Before Bator could finish what he was saying, the Prince, now trembling with anger, yelled to his guards. "Hurry up, throw him into the well!" Several lackeys seized Bator and took him away and before he had time to utter another word he was hurled into the well.

Not knowing that Bator had been seized his mother waited all day for him in front of their yurt. The sun went down and still he had not returned from the hunt. The moon rose above the mountains but still Bator had not come. The stars faded and dawn lightened the sky but still there was no Bator. Stricken with fear for his safety his mother went to seek news of him. A kind-hearted maid servant told her that Bator had made the Prince angry and that he had been bound and thrown into the prison. His mother rushed everywhere seeking help, and even personally begged the Prince to release her son. Day and night she cried, her tears flowing as freely as the waters of the river, but her Bator never returned. She did not know that her son had already been thrown into the well.

When Bator regained consciousness he had no idea how long he had been in the well. He had been awakened suddenly by the sound of running water. Looking around he discovered that he was not in the well at all. He was lying under a tree beside a river. "What, am I not dead?" he wondered, and as a test he bit his thumb. It hurt so much that he knew he was still alive. When he sat up he saw that all of his wounds from the beating had healed. He was still wondering what had happened, when he saw a man crouching on the earth, as if listening to something below the ground. First he put his right ear to the ground and then his left ear. It looked so strange to Bator that he went over to the man and asked, "What are you doing?"

"I am a house serf of the Netherworld Prince. I heard that Ulan Bator was in trouble and had come to this Kingdom. I want to befriend him."

Then Bator asked: "What magic power do you have to help him?"

The serf stood up and answered, "When I put my ear to the ground I can hear what is being said on the other side of the mountain. I'm called the Serf Who Can Hear from Afar. Who are you?"

"I'm none other than your friend Ulan Bator."

This made the Serf Who Can Hear from Afar extremely happy and he invited Bator to his home. Bator thanked him but said: "A lamb does not leave its mother, and I, Bator, cannot stay away from my native land. I cannot rest as long as my enemy is still alive. My mother is waiting for me and I must hurry home."

The Serf Who Can Hear from Afar, feeling that there was no other way, promised to send Bator back to the surface of the earth again. He told Bator to close his eyes. Bator obeyed and immediately felt himself rising, and heard the wind whistling in his ears. A moment later he heard someone whisper: "Bator, Bator, my friend, when you are in trouble, call me three times and I will come to your aid."

Bator opened his eyes and found he was once more on the surface of the earth, but not on the grasslands near his home.

In front of him stood a huge mountain. Looking down on the ground Bator saw that an arrow had been drawn there. He went in the direction in which the arrow was pointing, but he wondered how he would ever get home with so many great mountains blocking his way. As he walked he noticed that one of the mountains was moving. He thought this very strange and hastened forward to look more closely. To his great surprise he saw a man pushing the mountain ahead of him. Bator caught up with him and asked, "What are you doing?"

The man looked at Bator and without stopping what he was doing answered, "I'm a serf belonging to the Mountain Prince. I heard that Ulan Bator was in trouble and had come to the Mountain Kingdom. I should like to befriend him."

Bator asked, "What magic power have you to help him?"

The man stopped pushing the mountain and replied: "I am so strong that I can push mountains. I'm called the Serf Who Moves Mountains. Who are you?"

Bator said: "I'm none other than your friend Ulan Bator."

This made the Serf Who Moves Mountains very happy and he invited Bator to visit his home. But

Bator was anxious to return to his own home. So, the Serf Who Moves Mountains was obliged to send Bator to the other side of the mountains. He told Bator to close his eyes and as a gust of wind sent him sailing along Bator heard a cry like that of a beast. When the howling stopped a voice said: "Bator, Bator, when you are in trouble, my friend, call me three times and I shall come."

Bator opened his eyes and the mountains were now behind him but directly in front was a vast lake. "Such a big lake," he said to himself, "I shall never be able to swim across it!" Just then he noticed that the water of the lake was receding before him and finally it completely disappeared leaving the bed of the lake quite dry. Joyfully Bator ran forward. As he ran and ran, behind him the water rose again. Bator was really puzzled. Looking around he saw a man sitting among some reeds with a reed pipe in his mouth. Each time he breathed in the water was sucked up, and each time he breathed out, the lake water rose again. Bator called to the man and asked: "What are you doing?"

The man looked at Bator and continuing to use his pipe he answered: "I'm called the Serf of the Lake. I am a serf of the Prince of the Seas. I heard that Ulan Bator was in trouble and had come to the Sea Kingdom. I want to befriend him. Who are you?"

"I am none other than Ulan Bator your friend."

The Serf of the Lake was so glad to hear this that he invited Bator to his home. But when he saw how anxious Bator was to return to his own home the Serf of the Lake felt obliged to send him on his way to the other side of the lake. He told Bator to close his eyes. Bator did this and felt as if he were being rocked in a cradle, with the sound of the waves beating in his ears. After a time everything was quiet except for the whispering of a man who said, "Bator, Bator, whenever you are in trouble, my friend, call me three times and I shall come."

When Bator opened his eyes the lake had disappeared and before him lay the vast grasslands. As soon as Bator saw this he knew that his home was not far off and he went on his way happily. He walked and walked until the sun lay low on the horizon but still he didn't stop. Suddenly a bright streak of light appeared in front of him. It was a very strange light. He was a man who could recognize the flickering light of fireflies and the flashing green light of tiger eyes, but he had never seen a light such as this before. Standing there he pondered and pondered what it could be. Then Bator heard the neighing of a horse followed by the sound of several snorts. He laughed happily, for a horse to a herdsman is like water to a fish. Bator ran to where a white horse stood, its coat shining like silver. He mounted the horse and tried to ride off, but the horse shook its head, neighed again and refused to move. What was wrong? Bator looked carefully and discovered that each of the horse's feet was tied to a stake with a leather thong. Having no dagger with him, Bator got down on his knees and bit through them with his strong teeth. He did this until his mouth bled and his tongue bruised but he didn't give up. After he had bitten through the first thong, without even stopping to straighten his back, he started on the second. . . . At last he had severed them all. The silver horse flicked its tail, neighed, circled around Bator and then kneeled down before him. Bator said: "Oh beautiful silver horse, allow me to ride you home." The horse nodded three times and blinked his eye in approval. Bator leaped on its back, closed his eyes and all he could hear was the howling of the wind. Suddenly the wind dropped and he heard a voice say, "Return evil for evil and repay kindness with kindness. When you are in trouble call me three times."

Bator opened his eyes, the silver horse was not there but he found himself standing at the door of his own yurt. Bator's happiness was beyond words. He rushed inside to find his mother staring at the wall of the yurt. Her face had become haggard from grief and her hair had turned completely white. Bator immediately fell on his knees before her and announced, "Mother, I'm back."

Everyone was happy at Bator's return. They thought that the Prince had freed him out of pity. Bator said nothing but remained at home, sharpening his sword every day. News has wings! The report of Bator's return soon reached the Prince. He did not believe it and sent a man to confirm the story. The runner returned and reported that Bator was at home, was in good health, and that he was sharpening his sword. The Prince was amazed at the information. Had not he with his own eyes seen Bator thrown into the well. Since everyone was saying that he had set Bator free, the Prince could not very well arrest him openly.

Bator had thought that when the Prince heard he was back he would send his men to seize him. But when one day and then two days passed and nothing happened Bator became impatient. He suddenly thought of the Serf Who Can Hear from Afar. That night, when his mother had fallen asleep, he whispered: "Serf Who Can Hear from Afar, Bator is in distress and seeks your help." Suddenly the ground cracked and out stepped the little man. Then he pressed his ear against the ground and listened. Leaping up he whispered to Bator "Bad news! Bad news! The Prince has ordered his soldiers to wrap the hoofs of their horses in cotton so as to muffle the sound. They are to come and capture you tonight. Run away. Hurry!"

Bator thanked the Serf Who Can Hear from Afar and, hastily slinging his bow over his shoulder, he took up his sword and waited at the door. As he expected, a few moments later dozens of horsemen noiselessly rode up. Bator hid in the shadows while the horsemen dismounted and surrounded the yurt. Suddenly he yelled and leaped out. Brandishing his sword he slashed several of the guardsmen to pieces, but realizing that the odds were too great and fearful of his own safety Bator grabbed one of their horses and escaped.

The Prince's soldiers were soon in hot pursuit. When the Prince himself realized that Bator had escaped he mounted his fastest horse and joined the chase. While riding on Bator turned and aimed at the pursuers with his bow and arrow. Each arrow hit its mark, bringing down one after another of the soldiers from his horse. Soon Bator had used all his arrows but some guards were still following him. He rode like the wind until he found his path blocked by a huge mountain. At that moment Bator thought of the Serf Who Moves Mountains. He whispered three times, "Serf Who Moves Mountains, Bator is in trouble and seeks your help." With a roar the great mountain moved aside and Bator galloped on. A loud rumble was all he heard, and as he turned he saw that many of the Prince's soldiers had been unhorsed and injured by rocks which had rolled down the mountain. But some of them managed to escape and continued to chase him.

He rode on until a river blocked his path. Bator thought of the Serf of the Lake. He chanted three times, "Oh Serf of Lake, your friend Bator is in trouble." Swiftly the river was drained of its water and Bator dashed across. Immediately the river filled with water again and many of the pursuing soldiers were drowned. Only the Prince's horse had been fast enough to dash across in time. Bator reined in his horse, turned around and headed back towards the Prince.

When he saw Bator's gleaming sword the Prince tried to escape along the bank of the river. He was mounted on his famous red horse. Bator pursued him for a long time but fell farther and farther behind. Then he thought of the silver horse. Three times he called, "Silver Horse, Bator begs your help." He heard a neigh and the horse appeared at his side. He leaped upon it. The silver horse galloped and the wind whistled past Bator's ears. And in no time at all he had overtaken the Prince. Seeing that Bator had caught up with him the Prince was so terrified that he became powerless. Bator reached out, dragged the Prince closer to him, held him up in the air and then dashed him to the ground. The Prince begged and pleaded for mercy, Bator leaped down from his horse. With his foot pressing on the Prince

to hold him down he slashed him to pieces. . . . Bator then stuck his sword in the ground and after bowing three times to the heavens, said,

"Father, your son has avenged your death! My friends, all of you who were killed by the Prince, Bator has avenged your death!"

The sun gilded the surface of the river. Bator scooped up a handful of water, slacked his thirst, then leaped on to his horse and rode away.

The Seven Sisters

(A Miao Story)

One starry, moonless night seven wolves transformed themselves into seven young men and went down the mountain-side in search of food.

On the side of the mountain there lived seven maidens who spent most of their time at home spinning. The seven wolves saw the seven girls through a chink and banged on the door of their house. When the girls saw these strange faces they dared not open the door. Then the wolves shouted to them, "We need food and are on our way to find a cow to eat but we have lost our way. May we put up here for the night?"

The sisters answered: "It would be very inconvenient because our parents are away. Please go on to some other house."

"Well, we won't stay the whole night, but we need to sit and rest for a while, may we do that?" pleaded the wolves.

Hearing this the sisters felt obliged to open the door and invite their guests in.

When the eldest sister offered their guests chairs to sit down she discovered that they all had tails. She was very frightened, and without saying a word she slipped out of the house.

When the second sister gave the guests some water to drink she saw that their hands were covered with fur. She was also very frightened, and without warning the others, she too slipped out of the house.

As the third sister poured water into a basin for the guests to wash their feet, she noticed that their feet were covered with fur. She, too, was frightened and without saying anything, she also slipped away.

The fourth sister offered the guests some rice cakes. She noticed the ten little holes made in each cake by their claws. It frightened her so much that she dropped the cakes on the floor.

The wolves did not sit on the chairs which had been offered them. Nor did they drink the water, wash their feet or eat the rice cakes. Instead they stepped forward and asked the girls, "What's the matter with you?"

The fourth sister wanted to scream and run away, but she was too afraid to do either. She simply picked up the rice cakes and went back to her spinning.

Then the seven wolves sat down, drank some water, began to wash their feet and eat the rice cakes.

The whirring of the spinning-wheel was like the tender sighing of a woman. While she wept, the fourth sister whispered to her fifth, sixth and youngest sisters: "They are wolves that have changed themselves into young men. They will eat us!"

The younger sisters began to sob because they were too afraid to cry aloud.

The youngest sister said to the sixth sister, "You are older than I, you must save me."

And the sixth sister turned to the fifth sister and said: "You are older than I. It's your duty to save us."

The fifth sister, not knowing what to do, turned to the fourth sister and said, "You are older than I. You must think of a way to save us all."

The fourth sister knew that they could not run away from these beasts, but must think of some way to trick them. So she said to her fifth, sixth and youngest sisters, "Our three elder sisters only thought of their own safety. Since they have run away without warning us, we must think of a way to save ourselves. Each of us must try to think of something or we shall all be eaten by the wolves."

The fifth, sixth and seventh sisters agreed with what the fourth sister said. They continued to spin while they went on discussing the problem.

The spinning-wheel no longer sounded like the sighing of a sorrowful woman. The sisters cried no more, for they had thought up a clever idea. The fourth sister stood up and spoke to the guests, "We're so sleepy. Are you ready to leave now?"

The seven wolves answered, "It's early yet. Besides, you cannot go to sleep before your other sisters return. Come and warm yourselves by the fire."

The fourth sister seized this opportunity, saying, "That's right. We'll warm ourselves before going to bed. I'll go upstairs and fetch some more firewood."

The seven wolves saw nothing wrong in this and let her go upstairs.

A short time afterwards the fourth sister called to her other three sisters, "You'll have to come up and give me a hand. I can't bring it all down by myself."

So they too went upstairs.

After the seven wolves had finished eating and drinking and washing their feet, they gathered round the fire to warm themselves while waiting for the four sisters to come downstairs.

After waiting for a long time for the sisters to return, they grew impatient, and decided to go upstairs to search for the girls.

The eldest wolf went upstairs first and that was the last the other wolves ever saw of him.

Then the second wolf climbed the stairs and disappeared without a sound.

Following his disappearance the third went up and never returned.

The remaining wolves, the fourth, fifth, sixth and seventh, were completely baffled. They sensed that something had gone wrong and that it was not wise to go upstairs one by one. So each holding the tail of the one in front they ascended the stairs, the eldest among them leading the way.

Just as the leading wolf reached the top of the stairs he saw the sisters holding gnarled oak cudgels, stained with blood, high above their heads. Before he could yell out, the cudgels came down on him with such force that his head was split open. He tumbled backwards down the stairs, dragging the other three along with him. They rolled into the fire, scorching themselves and singeing their fur.

The three remaining wolves howled with pain and ran outside to cool off. The sisters rushed downstairs and bolted the door.

The three wolves realized that they had been tricked and that their four brothers had been killed. The more they thought about it the more angry they became. They changed back into their original form and tried to break open the door to avenge their brothers. They hurled themselves at the door, clawed

at it and howled, but the door withstood their onslaughts and all their efforts were in vain.

The spinning-wheel was humming once again but this time it sounded like a soft chuckle of satisfaction!

The wolves rushed round to the back of the house. They thought that it might be possible to break in through the back door and eat up the sisters who were spinning. But the back door was also firmly locked. Even if they had changed themselves into thin, pointed needles it would still have been impossible for them to get in. So they wandered around the courtyard and howled.

As they ran around, the fifth wolf saw a barrel with the lid slightly raised. There, exposed at the top of the barrel was an ear with an earring in the lobe. So he bit off the ear and scampered away. It was the ear of the eldest sister, who had hidden herself in the barrel in such a hurry that, without knowing it, she had left one ear exposed. The loss of her ear caused her to cry bitterly.

The sixth wolf ran around until he spotted a naked foot dangling from a tree. He leaped up, bit off a toe and then ran off.

It was the toe of the second sister, who had hidden in the tree. She was so frightened that she was unable to keep her balance and one of her feet dangled in mid-air. Fortunately she managed to draw up her foot in time and only lost one toe and not her whole foot.

Whirling around the place the seventh wolf saw a girl's leg in the bushes. He rushed over and had a bite at it before scampering away.

That was the third sister who had hidden her head in a bush, and like an ostrich, forgotten to hide the rest of herself. Now with a bite out of the top of her leg, her blood dripped everywhere. It was more than a year before she was able to sit on a bench again.

Thus the three elder sisters, because they were timid and selfish, paid a heavy price for their folly.

The fourth, fifth, sixth and seventh sisters, because they worked together, were able to think of a way to kill the wolves. And, what is more, each of them was able to add a fine fur to her dowry.

How Panpipes Came to Be Played

(A Miao Story)

In a Miao village there once lived a man and his wife whose names were Kaochio and Weiniao. The couple were over forty years old before their marriage was blessed with a child, a girl. When she arrived they were overjoyed, and called her Pangkao. Pangkao grew up to be clever and very deft with her fingers; at needlework, she outshone all the other girls in the village. She had slender, arched brows, bright eyes and cheeks like peach blossoms in the spring. When she decked herself out in her finery, people said she was more beautiful than a peacock. She was gifted also with an enchanting voice, and at the sound of her singing the most melodious songbirds were silent. Many young men in the village sought her hand in marriage, but Pangkao refused them all.

Whom, then, did this young maiden love? The truth was, she had already given her heart to a brave young hunter by the name of Mousha.

Mousha was a tall, strong, handsome young man who had once killed a tiger single-handed. At the time, it happened he was out hunting with his father in the forest. A tiger sprang out of a thicket and, growling fiercely, leapt upon the old man. Acting quickly, Mousha drew his knife and stabbed the tiger. The beast left the old man, now lying on the ground, and flung itself upon Mousha, who swung round and struck the tiger a forceful blow upon its head. The tiger reeled, then charged again, but the blow had weakened it considerably and finally, after stabbing it several more times in the head and body, Mousha finished him off. But Mousha's father, who had been badly mauled by the tiger, died, leaving Mousha and his dog to hunt alone in the hills.

One day Mousha wandered into a village, and to his surprise saw only cows and sheep there and not a single duck or chicken. When he asked the villagers about this they told him that there were two great birds of prey nearby, whose claws no duck or chicken could escape. Besides, these two birds had acquired magic powers and were so formidable that no one was able to cope with them. Mousha could hardly believe this, and said, "Is there really no way to deal with these creatures? Let me try." Bow and arrows in hand he followed the villagers to the lair of the bird monsters. Presently both of them flew out, their wings spread out like large mats. The birds were

as swift as arrows in flight, but no matter how fear-
some to look at and how swift in flight they were,
they could not escape the deadly arrows of Mousha.
He took his stance. His first arrow felled one great
bird and the second arrow killed the other bird. The
villagers were overjoyed and thanked this brave and
skilful hunter.

Now this event had happened in the village where
Pangkao lived, and when she saw this young, manly
hunter she fell deeply in love with him. But the
homeless Mousha, who was always wandering from
place to place, left the village the very next day.
How was he to know that there was a beautiful
maiden in the village who was sighing her heart out
for him? Mousha went away before Pangkao could
tell him of her love, but her thoughts went with him
into the hills.

As all young maidens in love do, Pangkao changed,
becoming more and more beautiful every day. Suitors
flocked to her door, but she refused every one, and
all they could do was to sigh in sorrow and turn away.

There is a saying, "Demons covet everything that
is good." And the beautiful, young Pangkao did not
escape the attention of a demon. In those parts there
was a white pheasant sprite who cast lustful eyes on
Pangkao. Knowing that he could never win her
heart, he plotted to capture her. One day while
Pangkao sat sewing she fell into a swoon and was

wafted away by a great gust of wind. Her parents were broken-hearted at their loss and wept grievously for her. The peasants were very distressed too and they searched high and low for her. But she had vanished without leaving a trace.

As for Mousha, he trekked through the forests, scaled many mountains and penetrated deep ravines, tracking down wild beasts. One day he came to a very dense forest and there he met a group of woodcutters of Han nationality. How good it was to find company in this lonely place! They spoke to Mousha, asking him his name and where he came from. Mousha saw that they were honest men and said, "I roam from hill to hill and live by hunting wild beasts. I am a wanderer without a home." The woodcutters took a liking to this young man and asked him to stay the night with them.

Sitting beside the bonfire after darkness had descended Mousha said to them, "Friends, tell me something about this forest!" And so they told him of their life and the wild animals that lived in the forest. Then they sighed and said, "Ah, this is a fine place, but we can't live here any longer." When Mousha asked them why, they replied, "A curse has come upon this forest. A terrible white pheasant sprite haunts it. Every night at the third watch it perches on the highest branch of yonder big tree and makes a blood-curdling screech. At the next watch

42

it moves to the second highest branch and screeches a second time, and just as dawn is breaking it screeches again from the third highest branch. What is even more disturbing is that we can always hear the sound of a young woman sobbing. These strange happenings are too much for us and we have decided to leave this abominable place."

Mousha realized at once that some monster was dwelling in the forest and he resolved to get rid of it. "Don't be afraid," he said to the Hans. "Tonight I shall watch and see what happens."

Shortly after midnight, when it was pitch darkness, Mousha and the others hid behind the big tree. They waited for a long time, then at the third watch, they dimly saw a monstrous white bird appear on the highest branch and heard it utter a shrill cry, exactly as the woodcutters had described. At the same time they heard the heart-breaking sobs of a young woman, borne on the wind now loud, now soft. At dawn the monster screeched for the third time, and only then did the men see it clearly. Mousha's swift arrow flew from his bow straight into the breast of the monstrous bird. The monster fell like a rock into the gully below, and the sobbing ceased. When it was broad daylight Mousha went down into the gully and found the body of a huge white pheasant. He was glad to have wiped out this evil monster, though he did not then know why a young woman had been sobbing. Plucking a feather from the tail of the white pheasant, he stuck it in his turban as a souvenir. In the morning he took leave of the wood-cutters and again set out.

When Pangkao returned home she told this story of her adventure.

After she had been carried away by the gust of wind she found herself imprisoned in a cave by an evil white pheasant sprite, who tried to force her to marry him. How could the lovely Pangkao submit to this! No matter how the white pheasant threatened her she only said "No!" All day long she cried to be released. Then the evil spirit, fearing she might escape, cast a magic spell over her so that she fell into a deep sleep each night. At dawn, when Pangkao awoke and resumed her sobbing, the pheasant screeched, and cast his spell over her again so that she would fall back into another swoon.

After the monster was killed, Pangkao awoke and ran out of the cave. She did not know where she was. But when she reached the edge of the forest she met the group of Han woodcutters, who were amazed to see her. They questioned her and learned that the cries they had heard every night were those of this pitiful maiden, and they realized that it was she whom the young hunter had set free. They told her what had happened the night before and every-one felt sorry that the young man had vanished. All they knew was that he wore a white feather in his turban.

Pangkao flushed with happiness when she learned that her rescuer was the same Mousha whom she loved. But where should she go to look for him? She had no idea! All Pangkao could do was to return to her village in the company of this group of kind-hearted woodcutters. Her old parents were overjoyed at the return of their beloved daughter. They embraced her fondly and through their tears said, "Daughter, tell us what has happened to you. Where did you fly to? We were so worried about you!" Pangkao told her parents the whole story of how she had been imprisoned and how Mousha had saved her. Then softly she poured out the whole story. "I love only him and now he has saved my life. I do not know where he is, but I will wait for him." Her old father's heart was glad, for he had seen Mousha and admired his bravery. But where was he wandering now? When would he come to the village again? These questions troubled both Pangkao and her parents.

Half a year passed without any news of Mousha. The maiden was pining away, waiting for her hero. One day the old father had a happy idea and said to his wife, "There is a way to find this young man!"

His wife was doubtful. "Where will you go to look for him?" she asked.

"We'll invite all the villagers around to a song and dance festival. Surely Mousha will hear of this and come." The father who was skilful with his hands, cut some bamboos, fastened them together and played a melodious tune on them. Then he showed the young people of the village how to make these panpipes and taught them how to play them. The more of these instruments they made the better they made them, and the more beautiful the tunes they played on them. At the Lunar New Year they held a festival of panpipes, at which they all sang and danced and made music. Not only did all the villagers come, but the people from the surrounding country-side all joined in, everyone dancing happily.

The dancing went on for nine days and nine nights. Then, on the tenth day, among the crowd Pangkao espied a young man wearing a white feather in his turban. She looked more closely. It was Mousha! The maiden's happiness knew no bounds and she rushed to tell her father, who invited Mousha to a feast.

Mousha did not know what it was all about and was going to inquire when the old man said, "My brave young man, once before you came here and helped us by destroying two terrible birds of prey. Now I want to ask you a question, where did you get the feather you are wearing in your turban?" Mousha was surprised at this question and wonder-

ed why the old man asked it, but he told him all that had happened in the forest. Then he said, "To this day I do not know why we heard the crying of a young woman or why the crying stopped when I shot down the white pheasant." Then Pangkao stepped from the inner room and gazed at Mousha through her tears. Her father told the young man the whole story and explained why they were holding the festival of the panpipes.

Mousha sympathized deeply with the beautiful Pangkao because of her cruel ordeal, and could not help loving her. And so the two were happily married.

This was the origin of the Miao people's panpipes festival. Or so they say. Also it was at that time that young Miao men and women began to wear a white pheasant's feather when they danced; in the first place to show that they were not afraid of evil spirits, and secondly because the wearing of the white pheasant's feather is supposed to bring them luck in love. But as white pheasant's feathers are scarce, Miao girls now wear instead, silver ornaments in the shape of a cock pheasant's tail.

How Aisu Found the Happy Land

(A Chuang Story)

In the village of Napo, where the sun rises, there once stood a tumbled-down thatched cottage beside the beautiful Tengtiao River. The occupants of this cottage were an old couple and their two sons, Aisa and Aisu. The elder son, Aisa, was a lazy lout who contributed little to the household. But, in spite of this, the family of four could have lived very well in this warm, fertile land, if not for misfortunes of one kind or another that ruined every harvest and forced them to live for long periods on wild roots and bitter herbs. The father fell ill, and because the family had no money to call in the medicine-man, they watched the illness grow worse, until they gave up all hope for his life. Yet the old man lay silent, uttering no parting words of consolation to his sons. Aisa, the elder son, whose sole concern was about money, asked his father time and again, "Pa, does anyone owe us anything?" The sick man did not answer, for he was wondering how it was possible for anyone to owe anything to a family as poor as theirs, which had not even an ox for the plough. Aisa is a silly ass to think of such a thing, he thought.

Then one day he summoned his two sons to his bedside and in a feeble, trembling voice said, "My children, I . . . I've thought again. There is someone who owes us a debt, owes our village of Napo a debt. Help me to sit up. It's easier to speak that way." Aisa and Aisu did as they were bidden, and their father continued, speaking with a stronger voice: "Once, not so many years ago, when the fields around Napo were golden with heavy ears of grain, the people in their rejoicing slaughtered pigs and oxen and held a feast till the whole village rang with their singing and joyful laughter. At the height of the merry-making catastrophe descended like a bolt from the blue — a great roar rent the heavens, sweeping away all songs and laughter. Darkness enveloped the hills and valleys. The land was devastated and the crops destroyed. That year, my children, a few people survived by eating roots and the bark of trees, but most of the villagers died of starvation. Now, do you know who brought this calamity? Who refused to let us live in plenty? It was the Thunder God. It is he who owes us a debt. My children, this debt must be exacted. I have no more to say." The brothers laid him down gently. He never rose again.

49

Aisu went to his mother and asked, "Ma! Is it possible to make the Thunder God pay this debt? Where can we find him?"

Aisa did not give his mother time to answer but replied for her: "Brother, you're dreaming. You should know the power of the Thunder God and not go against his will. To oppose him is only to invite trouble."

But the mother answered: "No, my children. Take courage — you can make him pay, and there is a way to do it. Moss is slippery and it is the Thunder God's mortal foe. Another thing, he's heavy and sinks easily into loose-ploughed earth. Be bold," she concluded, "and go forth bravely. You are sure to win."

Aisu encouraged by what his mother had said set out to carry out his task. First he spread a layer of moss over the cottage roof and, for want of an ox, he took his dog which strangely enough had nine tails instead of the usual one to help him plough the earth around the cottage to a great depth. Then solemnly, his heart filled with anger and grief, he wrapped his father's body in a mat and carried it to a marsh by the riverside, into which he threw it head first. The Thunder God, who was noted for his mischief-making, heard of this and flying into a rage, he bellowed: "Aha, young fellow, you who are so lacking in respect as to throw your own father into a marsh, are you ignorant of my power? I'll burn you to a cinder."

And with this he flew to the home of Aisu. Unexpectedly, however, he no sooner alighted on the roof than rolling down the slope he slid into the loose earth like so much horse manure. The Thunder God murmured, "I must get out of this," as he tried to get a foothold. But no matter how hard he tried to get up and run he could not extricate himself from the loose earth. He was struggling with might and main when Aisu arrived with a pair of tongs and grasped him tightly. The Thunder God raged and kicked, thinking to frighten Aisu, but the more he struggled the tighter the tongs closed on him. He bellowed himself hoarse but Aisu kept his hold on the tongs and said to him calmly, "So you've come, eh? Saved me the trouble of going up to heaven to find you. Now tell me. What about the debt you owe our village of Napo. It's time for you to pay up!"

The Thunder God screwed up his face feigning surprise and replied, "Aiya, when was I ever in debt to you? I never. . . ." Aisu did not wait for him to make his excuses but squeezed the tongs even tighter about the Thunder God.

"Speak up now," he commanded. "Are you going to pay or not!"

The Thunder God, feeling the pinching of the tongs, gave a loud roar and pleaded, "Pay! Pay! I'll pay. But I haven't a thing with me. Let me go and I'll send you something at once." Knowing that the

Thunder God had no intention of paying, Aisu squeezed the tongs so tightly that his prisoner had not enough breath left in his body to even shout. Then, when Aisu loosened his hold a little, the Thunder God, not daring to try any more trickery, came straight to the point: "All right, I'll let you have this magic cane."

"And of what use is that?" asked Aisu.

"It has great magic power over man. Strike a man with the head of the cane and he will fall dead, strike with the foot and he'll come alive again."

Aisu, unbelieving, replied: "Then why don't you strike me with your wonderful cane?"

"Look how securely you have me in your grip! I can't budge an inch."

Aisu, convinced now, took the cane from the Thunder God's grasp and warned him never again to commit evil. Finally he dragged the Thunder God out of the ploughed earth and let him go. Groaning, the Thunder God limped away.

When Aisu reached home with the cane, his mother was very happy because she knew that with this magic weapon he could perform many good deeds for the people. She praised her son for his prowess. Aisa had meanwhile taken fright and hidden in the pigsty. There he slept still trembling with fright until the pigs woke him up as they upturned the food trough.

The days flowed by, like the waters of the Tengtiao River, until it was three years since Aisu's father had died. Yet the family's livelihood had not improved. One night the mother called her sons to her and said, "My children, though the Thunder God has not visited us with any calamity for three years we still spend our days in misery. There is a place on this earth that is blessed and happy. Where is this place? You don't know, and your Ma doesn't know either. You must go and search for it, and if you are not afraid of difficulties you will certainly find it. Remember to follow the River of Clear Water and avoid the River of Muddy Water. And remember that when you pass your grandfather's grave on the wayside, you must not speak." Entrusting each of her sons with a sharp-edged sword, the mother added: "Take care on the way. Set out tomorrow, and when you have found this blessed land, don't forget to return for your kinsmen and friends here at Napo and lead them there."

The news spread quickly through the village, and relatives and friends gathered around the two brothers. Bonfires were lit and the village maidens danced and sang around them. The bonfires cast such a glow over the forest and the river that the birds, beasts and fish could not tell whether it were night or day. The singing and dancing continued throughout the night. At daybreak, the two brothers packed some rice cakes for their journey, said farewell to their kinsmen, and set off. Aisu took the Thunder God's cane, his nine-tailed dog and his sword.

Before noon they reached a grave mound. Aisa pointed to it saying, "Brother, this is our grandfather's grave." Just then their mother who had followed them approached, but the grave mound grew and grew until it blocked her way. She could only call to them, "Now my sons, because one of you disobeyed me and spoke I cannot accompany you any further. You will have to continue your journey alone. One thing you must remember, don't hit anything you find floating down the river. Now go!"

After two days' journey the brothers arrived at the place where the two rivers joined. The sun's rays from above scorched them like fire, and the hot pebbles on the shore of the River of Clear Water burnt their feet. Aisa, ignoring his mother's advice, turned to go along the Muddy River bank, because it looked as if it led to a cool, lush forest. The way was wide, smooth and altogether easier to take than that beside the River of Clear Water.

Aisa pointed to the scorching pebbles beside the River of Clear Water and said: "I don't see anything to be happy about there. Follow that for one day and you'll be half dead." Just then a plantain tree came floating by, borne along by the stream. Aisa unsheathed his sword and, before Aisu could prevent him, split it with one stroke. Blood gushed from the plantain tree, turning the water red. Aisu looked closer. He saw, alas, that it was their own mother that Aisa had struck and killed. Retrieving the body, they gave it proper burial. Aisu tried to persuade his elder brother to follow the River of Clear Water but, unable to do so, he took his magic cane and went his own way with his nine-tailed dog. He carried the dog over the scorching ground, jumping into the water after every few steps to cool off. He could not find so much as a blade of grass on which to sit and rest, so he proceeded without stop. At nightfall the going was easier and he continued to trudge on. After three days and nights, when the soles of his feet were covered with blisters, he finally reached the edge of a forest.

Continuing on his way, one day he came to a village where the people all looked sad. He thought this strange and asked an old man the reason for their gloom.

"Traveller," he answered, "great white tigers infest this place. They haven't harmed any people yet. They prefer cows and horses. They have eaten up all our livestock, and it won't be long before they'll start eating people. How can we avoid feeling downcast?"

Aisu said: "Old father, take heart, I'll rid you of these tigers."

Aisu went up into the mountains and found the tigers, but there were so many of them that he realized he could not cope with them all. Then an idea struck him. First, he would make friends with the tigers and spend the winter with them. When the days grew cold and the tigers shivered, Aisu said to them, "Friends, it's cold, but I know a way to keep everyone warm." Explaining what he would do, he asked them, "How will that suit you?"

The tigers all welcomed the idea. So Aisu bound dry grass around them with tendrils. It certainly made them feel much warmer. One day he caught one of the tigers off his guard, and he quickly set fire to his dry grass coat. The tiger roared with pain and rushed among the others, setting fire to one after another. They ran in all directions. Soon all of them had black sickle-shaped marks burnt in their fur. From that time there have been no snow-white tigers, all the young being born marked with this design. Moreover, since that time, no tiger has dared to make friends with man.

Aisu left the place and continued on his journey, working on the way in exchange for his meals. One day, after helping a family with the ploughing, he turned the ox out to pasture while he went to eat his own midday meal. The ox met a tiger who said, "Ox! How can you be so stupid as to let such a small creature as man dominate you?"

The ox replied: "I'm afraid you are quite wrong there; you don't know man's power, especially his craftiness."

"Aha, so he has a thing called 'craftiness'. I'd like to see it."

The ox said: "If you want to see it you can go and take a look. There is a man over there having his lunch."

The tiger, in his eagerness to see this thing called 'craftiness', forgot all about his experience with fire and ran to the shelter calling out to Aisu: "Man! I hear you have something called 'craftiness'; will you let me see it?"

Aisu thought, I am not inexperienced in dealing with tigers. Now that this fellow has come, I must give him a proper reception. "Why not?" Aisu answered the tiger. He placed his plough on the ground head up and, pointing to it, said to the tiger: "Please sit down. After I have finished my meal I'll show you this 'craftiness'."

As the tiger sat on the plough, the share pierced it's flesh. It wriggled about but didn't say a word.

"Eh," remarked Aisu, "can't you sit still a little while? Why are you fidgeting about? I'll show it to you directly."

So the tiger just sat and endured the pain till Aisu had finished his meal. Then he took a tether and said to the tiger: "Come, my friend, I'm going to show you what 'craftiness' is. Just lean against this big tree. That's fine. Now don't move!" Aisu bound the tiger to the tree and clubbed him over the head. The tiger cried out, "Enough . . . I don't want to see your 'craftiness' after all."

Aisu paid no heed but went on beating him, and the tiger was half dead before he was able to break loose. The ox laughed and laughed at the sight of the miserable tiger. It didn't dare even to look at the man but ran desperately into the forest. From that time onwards tigers have feared men and keep their distance.

Aisu resumed his journey and, after three days and nights, approached a village which at first sight appeared to be a lively place. When he entered, however, he found it empty and so quiet that he could hear a pin drop. After wandering around the village until dusk, he entered a deserted house and prepared to pass the night there. When he began to right an overturned tub which he saw on the floor, to his surprise, he found two beautiful maidens crouching in it. They were startled and happy to see Aisu and said to him, "Stranger, where have you come from and where are you going? Go quickly. You cannot stay here."

When Aisu asked why, the younger sister told him, "There is a man-eating monster here whose body is covered with long hair, whose fingers are as thick as the fruit of the plantain and whose eyes are like hen's eggs. Each morning it grabs someone, drags him by the hand and laughs. It eats the man at sunset, then goes back to its lair. All the people except we two sisters have been gobbled up. We have been hiding in this tub for three days, otherwise we too would have been devoured. The other members of our family are all gone. Brother, take us with you!" The sisters cried as they pleaded with him, but Aisu replied, "No, I can't take you with me, but I won't leave till I've killed this monster with my sword."

"Impossible! We had people whose swords were sharper than yours, but none could cope with the monster and all have been eaten by it. Please take us with you and leave this place quickly!"

Aisu ignored their pleading and prepared to pass the night there. With his sword, he cut two lengths of bamboo stem big enough to slip over his arms.

At daybreak, after the two sisters had crawled back into their tub, Aisu took his nine-tailed dog, buckled on his sword, slipped the bamboos on his arms, and with the Thunder God's cane in his hand went out. No sooner had he closed the door behind him than he heard the sound of weird laughing and looked up. Aiya! he saw a terrible monster! It had dishevelled hair reaching to its hips and a set of red teeth as long as chopsticks. Aisu neither moved nor showed any agitation when the monster drew near. It seized his bamboo-sheathed arms and with a chuckle, turned towards the rising sun.

"Ha, ha! I'll feast at sundown. Ha, ha! I'll feast at sundown," the monster kept repeating. The nine-tailed dog leapt at the monster, taking one bite after another out of its flesh. But the monster did not mind at all. For no sooner had the dog taken one bite of flesh than another grew in its place. Aisu cautiously drew his arms out of the bamboo sheaths and struck the monster with the head of the cane, but as if nothing had happened, it went on laughing and gloating over the feast it expected to have at sundown. Aisu lopped off the monster's head with his sword. Lo and behold! It grew another. The monster flew into a rage at the sight of the bamboo sheaths in its hands and tried to strike Aisu on the head with them. Aisu dodged and the bamboo sheaths sailed over his head and struck a rock behind him, splintering into slivers of a hair's breadth. In the tussle that ensued, however, Aisu could find no way of quickly finishing off the monster. The bout continued, until at sundown, the monster was completely winded and bolted back into its lair. There, when a young monster clamoured for meat to eat, it answered, "Humph! What are you talking about! Today, out of nowhere, came a fierce devil who nearly beat me to death. But he was a stupid one, and didn't know enough to smear his sword with dog's dung and chicken's droppings; otherwise I'd have been done for."

Aisu, who had pursued the monster to its lair, overheard what it said and happily went back to smear his sword with dog's dung and chicken's droppings. The next day the monster appeared again and Aisu quickly killed it. Aisu, thinking that when you pull out a thorn you should make a clean job of it, entered the monster's lair. There he saw many vats. Aisu asked the young monster what was in the vats and was told, "Little fish my mother has salted." Aisu killed the young monster, tipped over the vats and found that they contained not fish but the fingers of human beings. He struck these with the foot of the Thunder God's cane and hey presto, they changed into live men.

Aisu told these men what had happened. In their thanks to him, they asked him to settle down with them. Holding him in high respect, they elected him their chieftain. Aisu then married the younger of the two sisters. He had now found happiness and realized that this was the place of supreme joy that his mother had asked him to find. He decided to settle down.

Aisu had not forgotten his elder brother and after a time he went back to search for him. Passing through the forest and along the stony banks of the

River of Clear Water he came to the Muddy River. There he met a female monkey.

"Monkey! Have you seen my brother Aisa?" he asked.

The old female monkey just laughed. He asked again and she laughed once more. Aisu continued to walk beside the river until he found his brother, who asked him if he had met his sister-in-law on his way along the bank.

"I met no one," was his reply. "No one but a female monkey. When I asked her whether she had seen my brother she just laughed."

"Aiya! Brother, that was your sister-in-law."

Aisu was startled. "Really? So my sister-in-law is a monkey. Well, let's say no more about it. But come along with me. I've found the happy land."

"Fine!" replied Aisa. "But I have to fetch my children first. They're up there in that tree. I'll climb up and throw them down. Now be sure you catch them!"

Aisa climbed the tree and Aisu held out the skirt of his gown. But when he saw that the child was a monkey, he let it fall with a thud to the ground. So with the next three, till all four were dead. Before throwing down the fifth, Aisa pleaded: "Brother, spare the last child. Please do all you can to catch this one!" Aisu answered: "Yes, of course." But he let the fifth fall to its death, in the same way as the others had done. Tears of anger welled in Aisa's eyes, but after Aisu had pleaded with him for a long time Aisa finally agreed to go.

The two followed the course of the River of Clear Water to the happy land, Aisa grumbling all the way for having to walk on hot pebbles, till they finally arrived at their destination.

Aisu arranged a marriage between his wife's elder sister and his brother. But Aisa coveted his brother's wife for her beauty and plotted to get rid of Aisu. One day while they were out gathering bamboo shoots he pushed Aisu into a deep pit. When Aisa returned home he locked up his brother's wife, and attempted to force her to become his own. But Aisu's wife was a strong-willed woman and refused to submit to Aisa no matter how he tried to compel her to comply with his wishes.

The nine-tailed dog searched for his master in the bamboo grove for several days and finally found him. He lowered one of his tails into the pit, but when Aisu tried to pull himself up by it, the tail came off. The same thing happened with seven more of the tails, till only one was left, and this is why dogs have only one tail now.

At this Aisu said, "I can't get out of here this way. You keep your one tail, you'll need it to swat the flies. Fetch me a knife and a small bundle of bamboo."

The dog did as he was told and Aisu carved a number of pipes, which when blown made very sweet sounds. The music was so stirring that the birds all flocked around the pit, asking for the pipes.

"Do you really want them?" asked Aisu. He then pointed to a nearby bamboo saying, "Well, you can have them, but you must all stand on that bamboo until your weight bends it down into the pit. Then if I manage to get out I will give you all my pipes."

The birds bent the tree down as they were told. After Aisu had grasped the bamboo he asked the birds to fly away. The bamboo immediately sprang back, Aisu with it. The birds eagerly seized the pipes, and the different kinds of music made by the pipes have become their own ways of singing.

Aisa's plot to steal his brother's wife was foiled by Aisu's return. Then Aisa painted his bottom red, ran into a forest and transformed himself into a monkey because you see, he now had no face to see people.

Aisu and his wife were reunited and settled down in that fertile spot. The elders praised and loved him. The youth and children respected him.

Nor did Aisu forget his kinsmen and friends at Napo. He returned on a swift steed and the people there welcomed him with open arms. Unfortunately his mother was now dead. How happy she would have been to join in the welcome. He invited the villagers to the happy land and they all agreed to go. After three days of preparation they triumphantly set out for their destination.

Rice

(A Hani Story)

Long, long ago there was a kingdom where all the people lived on rice husks. Not knowing that the kernel of the rice was good to eat but believing it to be the "bone", they threw it away, and ate the husk, which they thought was the "meat" of the rice. In the king's palace were many servants, among them Miniya, a special maid to the Queen. The Queen was cruel and treated her maids abominably. If she was not ordering them to be beaten, then she was scolding them. Very often she did not give her maids sufficient food. One day, when Miniya was rather slow in carrying water to the Queen, she shouted at the young maid in an angry voice, "I feed you well but you serve me very badly. From now on, there'll be no food for you."

Miniya was forced to continue to serve the Queen but was given no food. As the days passed she grew thinner and thinner and her face turned as yellow as the dying leaves in autumn. Finally she reached the point where she could work no longer. She thought to herself, they won't give me anything to eat, but I can't just die like this from hunger without trying to do something about it. I'll try and chew the bone of the rice. She gathered up some grains of rice which had been thrown away and cooked and ate them. When she tasted the first mouthful she was very surprised. How is this, she said to herself. The bone is much better than the meat! And from then on, Miniya collected all the rice bones and stored them away, cooking some for herself every day. Many moons rose and then faded into the early dawn but Miniya did not die from hunger. On the contrary she grew more beautiful every day. Her face became as pink and as lovely as a rose in the fresh morning dew. The rest of the servants could not understand the reason for this change. Her soft, tender smile was so sweet that the men servants were attracted to her, like bees to a honeycomb.

One after another they slipped into her room and asked: "Miniya, how is it that you have become so beautiful when you have nothing to eat? Even the fairies are no match for you. Will you tell us your secret?"

Then Miniya told them that she had been eating rice bones. "For heaven's sake," she pleaded, "don't tell a soul, last of all the Queen."

So each evening the other servants slipped into her room, also ate their fill, and slipped away again.

When she saw how beautiful Miniya had become, the Queen was filled with envy. She thought that the King might take Miniya for his Queen instead of her. So the Queen, filled with hatred summoned Miniya before her. The Queen was cunning and pretended to speak kindly, "My dear little Miniya, you look so beautiful, tell me what you do to make yourself so attractive and I will give you anything that your kind little heart desires. Tell me, my dear little Miniya! I cannot bear to go on living if you don't. You're such a good girl, I know you have a heart of gold and you won't let me suffer like this."

The Queen thought that such flattery was sure to make Miniya part with her secret; then she too could become beautiful. But the Queen's shameless behaviour only made Miniya more annoyed. Not uttering one word, Miniya just stood there and looked at the Queen scornfully.

Seeing that she had failed in her attempt to obtain the secret, the Queen was upset for the rest of that day. That night the Queen twisted and turned restlessly on her bed with vexation.

Some days later, noticing the good relations between Miniya and the rest of the servants, and how much Miniya loved them, she thought of a wicked plan.

So the next morning the spiteful Queen shouted at Miniya, "If you don't tell me your secret, you wretch, I'll ask the King to have every servant in the palace put to death."

Miniya hid in her room and wept until her eyes were red and swollen.

When the other servants saw her crying they asked: "Miniya, what's troubling you so much that you cry so bitterly? Tell us. We'll help you. Has the Queen had you beaten again?"

But Miniya did not answer, and continued to weep as though her heart would break. Her friends then wept with her. Miniya could not bear to see her friends weep, so she told them the truth. "The Queen says that if I don't tell her what has made me so beautiful, she's going to ask the King to have you all killed. That is why I'm so sad."

When the servants heard this, they were filled with indignation and cried out together, "Don't tell her your secret! If she wants to have us killed, then let her do it!"

"But I cannot see you all die for such a small matter," Miniya protested.

"We would rather die than let her know the secret," the servants said with great determination.

But how could Miniya allow her friends to be put to death? She thought and thought and finally found a way to deal with the Queen and at the same time

69

protect her friends. She ran to the Queen and whispered, "My good Queen, I'm ready to tell you what I do that makes me so beautiful. But this is not a convenient place to talk about such an important thing. Let's find some other place to talk. Wait, we had better go to your room. We can talk there and no one will overhear us."

The Queen led Miniya to her room, remarking with great pleasure, "Miniya, I've always said that you were both kind and beautiful. Quickly, tell me what you would like as a reward in exchange for your secret and I'll see that you have it."

A smile hovered over Miniya's beautiful face and the Queen, seeing its loveliness, could hardly wait to be as beautiful as this little maid. She urged Miniya to be quick and tell her the secret.

"My good Queen," cautioned Miniya. "Be patient. I promise to tell you. I don't want any reward, but I have one request to make," Miniya stated gravely.

"Of course, of course! Tell me and I'll see that your request is granted. Hurry up now and tell me, my sweet little Miniya."

"You won't break your promise?"

"No! No! Miniya. Quickly, tell me."

"Now you have promised, you must carry out my request. You must do as I ask before I tell you my secret. Please ask the King to release all the servants and never have them in the palace again."

So the Queen went to see the King and after much persuasion finally persuaded him to do it. He then gave the order for all the servants to be set free. When Miniya saw that all her friends had safely left the palace, she turned to the Queen, smiled and said, "My good Queen, now I will tell you my secret. Do you remember when you forbade me to eat? I was very hungry for the first few days and found life very difficult to bear, but I persisted in my efforts to keep alive and then slowly I began to grow more and more beautiful. I regained my weight and felt very well. My Queen, if you will persist and do as I did, you will become even more beautiful than I am."

The wicked Queen was so anxious to be beautiful that every day she willingly suffered the pangs of hunger. After ten days or more had passed the wicked Queen died of starvation. The King, now without servants to wait on him, also died.

Thenceforth the Hani people tilled their land and ate fragrant white rice. And to this very day whenever they cook a pot of delicious steaming rice they recall this story from the distant past.

The Suit of White Feathers

(A Tunghsiang Story)

Long, long ago among the Tunghsiang people there lived a girl called Fatuman, whose mother died when she was very young. Her stepmother was an evil woman who was always thinking of ways to torment the poor child. Fatuman was a very clever little girl and no matter how difficult the task her stepmother set for her, she always did it perfectly. But because her stepmother could find no fault in her, she grew to dislike her even more. She thought, "The only way I'll ever have any peace is by getting rid of this troublesome girl!"

On Fatuman's thirteenth birthday her wicked stepmother sold her to an evil, black-bearded man for fifty taels of silver. It was agreed that in three days he would come and take her away to marry her.

Then both the front and back doors of the house were locked, and there was no way of escape for poor Fatuman. She was like a young fawn which has fallen into a pit: panic-stricken, distressed and helpless!

High in the sky a flock of doves flew by and Fatuman, looking through the window and seeing their free and happy flight, envied them. Sitting beside the window she softly sang,

> *Oh doves so white, oh doves so white,*
> *How I admire your swift flight.*
> *If only a pair of wings had I,*
> *I'd willingly fly into yonder sky!*

That night she dreamed that the flock of doves alighted around her bedside.

One of the doves spoke, "Little maiden, we have some gifts for you. Take them and make yourself a suit. If you need to escape in time of danger, put it on and fly away to freedom and happiness."

Having said this, one by one the doves pulled several feathers from their plumage, placed them on Fatuman's bed, and then flew away.

The sound of flapping wings woke Fatuman from her dream. There beside her was a pile of feathers! She felt extremely happy. She lit her lamp, and doing as she had been advised by the doves, there and then started to make a suit for herself. With a fine needle and a skilful hand she worked watch after watch until finally, a white dress, beautiful and light, was made at dawn.

73

Two days passed and on the morning of the third day the black-bearded man, leading a horse, came to take his bride away! Fatuman was so frightened that she dared not go out and locked herself in her room.

Pretending to be kind, the stepmother stood outside the door and called:

"Open the door, my good daughter."

"I'm dressing, mother!" answered Fatuman.

A few minutes later the stepmother asked again:

"Have you finished dressing, my daughter?"

"I'm just combing my hair, mother."

A few more minutes passed and the stepmother was now somewhat impatient:

"Fatuman, haven't you finished yet?"

"I'd like to wash my face now, if I may!"

Several more minutes passed, and the stepmother, now very angry, shouted,

"Wretch girl, haven't you finished yet?"

"No, I'm putting on my dress!"

Her patience exhausted, the stepmother called the black-bearded man. He kicked open the door and they both rushed in. Fatuman was just putting on her soft, feathered suit. And before they could touch her, she suddenly changed into a white dove. Cooing, she flew through the doorway and soared into the sky. After circling around several times she flew out of sight. . . .

She flew on and on for a long time before alighting in the fork of a tree near a mountain path. The sun was then setting, and grief-stricken she sang a sad song,

> Coo, coo, coo, how can I be calm,
> My stepmother brought me too much harm.
> Friendless, amidst the clouds and sky,
> Where can I find a place to rest, O my?

As she sang, tears trickled from her bright eyes. At the end of the village street an old man, who owned a tea-shop, heard her sad song and sang to console her:

> White dove, oh dove so dear,
> Don't grieve or cry. Can you hear?
> Destiny has willed that we should meet,
> In my house, you will rest your weary feet.

The kind old man then placed three tea pots on the table, a gold one, a brass one and an iron one. He picked up the gold tea-pot, and from it he filled a jade cup with crystal clear water. Placing it on a table near the door he called to the dove in the tree:

"Little white dove, come and take a drink!"

The dove was very thirsty after flying for so many hours. Tempted by the old man's kindness, she overcame her fear and flew down to drink the

75

water.   Suddenly she quivered.   As the old man reached out to stroke the beautiful feathers of the dove, it changed into the maiden Fatuman. . . .

Fatuman asked if she might stay. He was pleased to have her company and so she remained at the shop and did odd jobs for the old man who was very kind to her.   In return he cared for her as he would have done for his own daughter.   Fatuman was very happy.

One day the old man said to her: "There are three pots on the tea table.   The gold tea pot is for immortals, the brass one is for ordinary people and the iron one is for evil people.   When you make tea for ordinary people, use the brass pot."

One day Fatuman took the pail and went to fetch some water.   Unexpectedly, she saw her stepmother and the black-bearded man coming up the hill. She was very frightened and hurried back to the house. Searching for her white feathered suit and stammering with fright, she told the kind old man, "A terrible thing has happened. . . .   My stepmother has come to find me!"

"Don't be afraid, my child," replied the old man. "You just sit quietly in the room. I know how to deal with them."

The wicked pair reached the top of the hill, then the shop.

"Old man," they asked. "Have you seen a strange girl around here? We have heard that she came to stay with you. Is that right?"

"The only stranger who has been here is a white dove. She sought shelter in my tea shop because someone was trying to harm her."

"That's her — she's my daughter," said the step-mother.

"That's her — she's my wife," cried the black-bearded man.

"Hurry up, old man! You must give her back to us immediately!" they shouted.

"Don't be in such a hurry, don't be in such a hurry!" answered the kind old man with a smile. "After chasing someone for such a distance in a hot weather like this, I'm sure you must be thirsty. Come, let us first have a cup of tea, then we can talk things over." And as he spoke, he took up the iron pot and poured out two bowls of tea. They had only taken a few sips from the bowls, when they both began to change into little smoky-grey birds. They flew down to the ground and began to chirp and hop about under the table. Waving his hands, the old man shooed them away. They flew out of the door and alighted in the fork of a tree. Laughingly, the old man called to Fatuman who was still hiding, "Come out my child. Look, the evil ones have flown up into that tree."

As soon as Fatuman went outside, the little smoky-grey birds in the tree raised their voices and chorused,

"Go home! Go home, wretched girl!"

"Go home! Go home, wretched girl!"

The old man picked up a stone and frightened them away.

A little later, when Fatuman was sitting by the stove boiling water the two birds returned and again chirped,

"Go home! Go home, wretched girl!"

"Go home! Go home, wretched girl!"

". . . . . !"

They kept up a constant clamour. Fatuman, becoming very uneasy, said to the old man:

"Please chase them away!"

He took a long branch and shooed the two noisy pests until they flew away. But again it wasn't long before they were back repeating their call,

"Go home! Go home, wretched girl!"

"Go home! Go home, wretched girl!"

". . . . . !"

"Oh hurry up, please drive them away," pleaded Fatuman. "Their constant chorus will drive me crazy."

The old man was busy at that moment kneading dough for bread. He pinched off a small piece and threw it into the air. It instantly changed into a sparrow-hawk. With a scream, the sparrow-hawk

78

flew straight towards the tree where the noisy couple was perched. The little grey birds were so frightened that they flew far away and never returned.

And to this very day, if you go deep into the forest, you can see these ugly little birds with smoky-grey feathers. The instant they land in a tree they cry out:

"Go home! Go home, wretched girl!"

"Go home! Go home, wretched girl!"

Their worst enemy is the sparrow-hawk. When he hears their constant clamour he chases them. And to this day the people call these small grey birds "seekers".

"Black Horse" — The Third Brother Chang

(A Tu Story)

Once upon a time there lived an old woman whose surname was Chang. In her younger days she had a son and a daughter and was quite well off. But, like all the other people of the neighbourhood she lived in constant fear, for nearby lived a nine-headed monster that ate human flesh and drank blood. Granny Chang's family had all been eaten by the monster and she was left sad and lonely, a black mare her only possession.

So month after month and year after year, her only company was this mare. When Granny cried, the mare wept; and when Granny was happy, so was the mare. One day Granny discovered that the stomach of her black mare was swollen, and thought that the mare might have eaten too much. But as time went by the mare's stomach grew larger. When the old woman pressed it gently she thought she could feel a movement inside. This filled her with joy and Granny had hoped that the mare would soon drop a lively foal. Day and night she anxiously waited. But in the end, instead of giving birth to a foal, the mare only dropped a queer sack of skin. Granny didn't know how such a strange thing could have happened. Sighing she muttered: "What bad luck! I've had a lifetime of nothing but trouble!" Not wanting to let her misfortune become known, the old woman buried the skin sack behind the stable wall.

Three days later, when Granny was feeding the mare, she noticed that the ground, where she had buried the skin sack, was quivering. Startled, she dug it up again and opening it with a knife, inside she found a plump baby boy.

This made her very happy and she named the boy "Black Horse" after his mother, the mare. The old woman loved the boy very dearly; she gave him the best of everything. He grew up strong and very clever. At the early age of five he already knew a great deal.

When he was a young man he saw Granny crying one day, and asked:

"Granny, what's wrong?"

Granny really did not want to tell the young man why she was crying, but as he insisted she finally gave in and answered, "Foolish young man, it's time you knew that your sister and brother were eaten by the nine-headed monster! How can I be happy when I think of them. . . ."

Granny told Black Horse all that had happened and insisted that he always remember it.

After Black Horse heard this he aśked Granny for a bow and arrows, which she gave him. Then one day, strapping his bow and arrows to his back, he said to her:

"Granny, you have taken good care of me, but I'm a man now, and I must go out into the world to find myself some brothers. . . ." Granny was worried for she felt that he was still too young to go off alone. On second thoughts, however, she decided that it was better to let him have his own way. So determined not to let him see her sorrow she wiped away her tears and saw him off.

A day's journey took Black Horse deep into the mountains. There he saw a huge rock that resembled a house. Fitting an arrow to his bow, he released it and the rock fell down on its side. Immediately a voice from under the rock cried out, "Which of my brothers has knocked over my house? Where are you going? Are you going up or down the mountain?"

"Neither," answered Black Horse. "I want you to come out and pledge to be my sworn brother."

At this a big man stepped from under the rock and asked, "Am I to be your elder brother or your younger brother?"

"As you come from under the rock you should be my elder brother," answered Black Horse.

They started off together and the elder brother asked, "Where are we going?"

"First we will go hunting on top of the mountain," answered Black Horse.

They climbed up and up, until they came to a tall pine tree. Fitting another arrow to his bow, Black Horse released it and knocked over the pine tree. Immediately a voice from under the tree asked, "Which of my brothers has turned over my house? Where are you going? Are you going up or down the mountain?"

"Neither," replied Black Horse. "Please come out. I want you to be my sworn brother."

At this a tall man stepped from under the tree and asked: "Am I to be your elder or your younger brother?"

"This is my elder brother, who came from under the rock; as you have come from under the tree, you should be my second brother. I am younger than you, so just call me Third Brother Chang," answered Black Horse.

From then on, the three became sworn brothers who shared life together, both its joys and sorrows.

The three brothers travelled far into the mountains until they came to a dilapidated hut in a valley where there was no sign of life. There they settled down to live. During the day time they hunted in the mountains, returning to the hut in the evening to sleep. They lived in this manner for a long time. One day the brothers returned to the hut, to find there a pot of freshly cooked, steaming rice. The fragrance of it filled the house. "How strange," exclaimed Black Horse. "We have never seen one single person in this valley. Who could have been here and cooked for us?"

The two elder brothers picked up their bowls and started to eat but Black Horse stopped them, saying, "Wait, don't be in such a hurry. Let me taste it first to see if there's anything wrong with it."

Black Horse tasted the rice and found it extremely good. So the three brothers ate all they wanted. There was just enough, neither too much nor too little.

The next day when they returned from hunting there was another pot of freshly cooked rice awaiting them. Once more the brothers ate their fill. Every day after this the rice was mysteriously prepared. Black Horse said: "Each day we go hunting without knowing who cooks our dinner. Tomorrow one of us should stay behind to watch the house."

"I'll stay behind tomorrow and watch," agreed the eldest brother. "I'll stand in the doorway; then I'll be able to see who comes in."

"Good," said Black Horse. "Tomorrow you stand watch."

The next morning the eldest brother posted himself at the door and waited. By noon he had not seen a sign of anyone. But when night fell and he went into the house to look around he saw a pot of steaming rice there. The eldest brother was astonished and filled with shame. As big as I am I failed to see anyone, he thought to himself. When his two brothers returned and saw how upset he was they did not question him. Later the second brother said: "Tomorrow I'll stand watch and see who comes in."

So the next day the second brother stretched out on the *kang* to keep watch. Unfortunately he soon fell asleep, and when he awakened it was dark and again there stood another pot of steaming rice. When his brothers came back they scolded him for his lack of vigilance. Black Horse said: "Tomorrow you go hunting while I watch the house."

On the third day Black Horse lay on the *kang* pretending to be asleep. Late in the afternoon three doves flew into the room through an open window. They immediately changed into three beautiful girls. One made the fire, the second one carried water and the third one prepared the rice. They finished everything in a few moments. When they were about to leave, Black Horse called out in a loud voice, "Don't be afraid. Tell me, where did you come from?" The girls were shy and very frightened, but the youngest of them was brave enough to answer. "We're fairies. We know that after a day's hunting you brothers are always tired, so we decided to come down and cook for you."

"Why do you wish to come here when heaven is so beautiful?" questioned Black Horse.

"Heaven is not so wonderful as being with you," answered the third sister, for her elder sisters were still too shy to speak.

"Then don't go back. Stay here and marry me and your sisters can marry my brothers. Will you do that?" pleaded Black Horse.

The three sisters nodded their approval. They blushed and hid their faces but they couldn't hide their joy. The two elder sisters were as beautiful as peach blossoms. The third sister was somewhat dark but as pretty as a plum flower.

When the other two brothers returned they called out: "Third Brother, did you have any luck today?"

"Yes. While I watched three beautiful girls came here and cooked our rice. Now they are willing to become our wives," answered Black Horse. "See how beautiful they are!" The two brothers looked and cried aloud with delight: "Third Brother, you are really marvellous!"

The sisters filled three bowls with rice, the eldest sister serving the eldest brother and the second sister serving the second brother, leaving the youngest sister to serve Black Horse. In no time at all they became three loving couples.

The youngest sister's skin became fairer and fairer each day until she was even prettier than her two elder sisters. Black Horse was really very fortunate. But when he thought of home and his grandmother he felt very sad at heart. One day he told his brothers that he wanted to go home and fetch the old woman. His second brother said: "Let me go for you. When I was given the task of watching the house I didn't do a good job. But with my long legs I can make this journey and return within a day. I promise you that I will carry out this mission, I'll carry her on my back." Since the eldest brother and the young wives all agreed that the second brother should undertake the task, Black Horse let him go.

The second brother with his very long legs was certainly a fast walker. Carrying the old lady carefully on his back he returned within a day as he had promised. Tears of joy flowed from Granny's eyes as she embraced Black Horse. It gave the old lady great joy to see that her son was well fed and clothed, and had a good wife and kind brothers.

But, not long afterwards, the nine-headed monster again appeared.

He came at a time when the brothers were away hunting in the mountains. "Ha, ha," he laughed. "There is plenty of meat here and now Granny has three beautiful daughters-in-law. Wonderful! What shall I do first? Gobble up all this meat or drink your blood?"

They were all dumb with fright, except for the third sister who said, "There's plenty of meat here. If you eat that first, you will still have plenty of time left to eat us."

"Yes, that is true! Anyway you won't be able to get away," growled the monster.

When the brothers returned Granny told them of the nine-headed monster's terrible visit. The eldest brother said: "Well, tomorrow I'll stand watch and slash him open with one blow."

"That's a good plan," approved Black Horse. "But Granny and our wives must not stay here in the house."

The next day the eldest brother sat in the doorway like a great stone. There he stayed the whole day but not even one glimpse of the monster did he see. Yet unknown to him the monster had entered by the back door and had eaten up some more of the meat and carried away some oil. That evening when they all returned they asked their brother, "Did you see the monster?"

"Curse it," he said. "I kept watch at the door all day and saw neither hide nor hair of him."

When they saw how much meat had been eaten the young wives asked, "But, how could you have missed him? See how much of the meat is gone!"

The second brother said, "Tomorrow I'll stand watch. I don't care how fast the monster can run. I'll drag him back."

Black Horse repeatedly warned the second brother that he should take great care not to fall asleep.

But the next day, having waited all the morning without seeing anything, second brother fell fast asleep. Again, the monster came, ate some of the meat and carried off more oil. When the others returned and found the second brother asleep they were angry with him. Then Black Horse declared: "Tomorrow I'll stand watch!"

So on the third day Black Horse took his sword and hid behind the door. Soon the nine-headed monster came into the house and roared: "Where are the beautiful sisters?" The words had hardly left his lips before Black Horse had cut off one of his heads.

"Aow, aow!" The monster howled in pain. "There's a terrible creature in this house." And turning around he swiftly fled.

Black Horse did not chase after him but picked up the head that he had chopped off and hung it up.

That evening his brothers, their wives and Granny returned and asked, "Black Horse, did anything happen during your watch?" "Look," answered Black Horse, "I cut off one of the monster's heads."

"My children," cautioned Granny, "weeds should be pulled out by the roots. The monster still has eight heads!"

"Don't worry, Granny! My brothers and I will make sure that we put an end to that monster."

That night Black Horse and his two brothers thought of a good plan. The following morning they put on their swords, said goodbye to their wives and Granny and went to look for the nine-headed monster.

As they went down the mountain they saw a village. Then they met a young shepherd.

"Shepherd boy, can you tell us where the nine-headed monster lives?" requested Black Horse. The boy answered: "It is I who take his sheep to graze. He is very cruel! Every day since he captured me he has beaten me. He forces me to wait on him."

"Never mind," said Black Horse. "Tonight you must lead us to his lair and together we will kill him."

The young shepherd cheerfully promised, saying, "For the last two days the nine-headed monster has been trying to cure his wound. Every night I have to bring him tea and dress his wounds. Tonight I'll take you to him and when he's off his guard you can kill him."

That night the three brothers hid themselves among the sheep and slipped into the lair of the nine-headed monster. The young shepherd led them into the room where the monster lived. The eldest and second brothers hid behind the door and Black Horse hid behind a cabinet. The nine-headed monster called for the shepherd boy to pour out some tea and dress his wounds. Just as the monster was relaxing, and feeling more comfortable Black Horse rushed up and cut off four heads.

"Horrible!" screamed the monster as he scrambled up and rushed out. But as he reached the door the eldest and the second brother rushed from behind it. They chopped off the rest of his heads with their swords. Then the three brothers stabbed the monster again and he finally breathed his last.

Taking the young shepherd boy with them the three brothers returned to the mountains. When their wives and the old woman heard that they had killed the monster they all cried with joy. And from that time on they have lived happily together in that place.

The Wooing of Pumei

(An Olunchun Story)

In ancient times, an old hunter, who had seen more than sixty summers, lived on the bank of the Kuerpin River. He had one son whom he called Yentsiao.

Early one morning, Yentsiao aimed an arrow and shot a white bird, which fell from the clouds into the river below. He rushed to retrieve the wounded bird from the rushing water but the swift current had already swept it away.

At that moment a girl with a red poppy in her hair appeared on the opposite bank. She was carrying a bucket made of birch bark, which she filled with water from the river. Then she looked up at Yentsiao and sang,

> Oh hunter by the Kuerpin River,
> Why do you look so sad?
> You're more powerful than an eagle,
> One day fortune will make you glad!

Yentsiao did not utter one word but drawing back his bow he shot an arrow into her bucket. Plugging the hole with her finger she called out: "That's neither brave nor clever. If you really want to show what kind of man you are, why don't you go and find your father's giant horse and ride him. Then you'd really win my admiration!" She turned and walked away towards the grey mountain.

When Yentsiao returned home he said: "Father, I'd like to find that great horse of yours and ride him." "Nonsense," replied his father. "He'll trample you to death. Many years have passed since I last tried to ride him." Yentsiao persisted and his father finally agreed. "All right," he said, "go to the big yellow rock beyond the Santao Ridge and look around till you see a wooden trough there. If there is no water in it then go and look for the horse among the reeds below the ridge. But, do be careful."

Yentsiao found the yellow rock. The giant horse, who had just finished drinking, came towards him. The horse's hoofs were as large as spinning wheels and its mane dragged on the ground. Standing beside the horse, Yentsiao in comparison, looked like a child. Involuntarily, Yentsiao backed away from the animal. But as he did so he thought, after all I came here to ride him, didn't I? It won't help me if I am afraid. Slowly he approached the big horse, but it tossed its mane and would not allow Yentsiao to come very near. Seeing that the horse was keeping out of reach, Yentsiao went around the edge of the reedy marsh and climbed up a pine tree and waited. Presently, the horse trotted under the tree. Yentsiao jumped down on to its back. The loud protesting snorts of the plunging horse shook the very mountain. Yentsiao took firm hold of the horse's mane and no matter how the horse bucked and reared he hung on as if he were glued to it. This went on for hours and by sunset sweat glistened on the horse's flanks. Finally Yentsiao tamed the horse and rode him home.

As he approached the bank of the river the girl with the red poppy in her hair was there once more, and again carrying water in her bucket. Without a word Yentsiao once more shot an arrow into her bucket. The girl looked up slowly and said, "I see! So you have found the horse. But there's nothing very brave or clever about that either. If you are man enough, then travel to the bank of the Panku River and look for a girl named Pumei. She's waiting for you. It's two thousand *li* from here. If you can endure the hardships along the way she will marry you and help to take care of your aging father. Well, see if you can do it!" Again the girl walked off in the direction of the grey mountain.

Yentsiao went home and said to his father: "Father, on the bank of the Panku River, there's a girl called Pumei waiting for me to take her as my bride. Let me go, and when she comes back with me, you'll have someone to take care of you." "You'll never find her," his father replied. "The road to the Panku River leads into an unknown country. Many people have set out to get there, and travelled part of the way, but all became afraid and turned back. If you have nothing better to do, go down to the river bank and catch some rabbits. Let others go to Pumei for a wife. It's late. Get some sleep and stop this foolishness!"

Yentsiao looked up at the starry sky. It seemed as if the stars were winking, and ridiculing him for losing face in front of a girl. The more Yentsiao thought about it the more determined he was to go. Just as the eastern horizon was turning pink, and while his father was still sound asleep, Yentsiao slipped out of the house. Then springing on his horse he rode off to find the Panku River.

Yentsiao crossed the Kuerpin River and arrived at the foot of the grey mountain. As he gazed at it he thought it strange that there wasn't a single tree on its slopes. Looking more closely at the mountain he thought it moved. Then he discovered it was not a mountain at all but the huge bulk of a dragon. Yentsiao hurriedly climbed up the sides of a nearby precipice to take another look. The dragon was coiled in a circle, in the centre of its coils were thirty-eight beautiful girls. Seeing Yentsiao mounted on his great horse they sang a chorus to him,

> *Caught here in a cruel snare,*
> *Our fate is as bitter as brine,*
> *Oh rider on the great horse over there,*
> *No longer waste your time!*
> *Will we ever see our families kind?*
> *We do not even know.*
> *Don't idle away your precious time,*
> *Oh hunter with a mighty bow!*

> *We've been brought here by the dragon,*
> *From places far and near,*
> *And though we're not your sisters,*
> *Please do not leave us here!*

Sympathetically, Yentsiao answered them with a song:

> *My sisters you are in peril,*
> *Your sorrow is also mine,*
> *If I fail to kill the dragon now,*
> *I'll try until I do — I vow!*

Bending his mighty bow with all his strength, Yentsiao aimed at the head of the dragon. Like a shooting star the arrow sailed through the air, cutting deep into the dragon's brain. Then Yentsiao, galloping his horse towards the young girls, called out, "It's all right, you're safe now!"

The life of the dragon ebbed slowly away, but at the last moment it roared aloud and a gush of black blood poured from its wound. "Aiya! it's scalding me!" Yentsiao cried out, the blood having gushed over him. He fell from his horse and lay beside it as if dead.

Quickly, the young girls gathered around and did everything they could to revive him. Taking a gleaming pearl from the dragon's head and placing it on Yentsiao's bloody chest, they sprinkled his head with cool water from a nearby spring. Then holding hands the girls circled round him and sang:

> *Awake brave hunter, awake and live,*
> *To us maidens you gave new life.*
> *If for this your life you give*
> *Sorrow will pierce us like a knife!*

. . . Yentsiao gradually opened his eyes and as he began to breathe deeply the pearl rolled to the ground. With the help of the girls he sat up and looked around. The girls smiled at him, and like most other young men would have done, he blushed and tried to escape. The girls called after him, "Come back! If you run away how can we repay you for saving our lives?" Then one of the elder girls said, "We owe our lives to you, and since we have no other way to express our thanks, we ask you to choose one of us for your wife."

"Don't worry yourselves about that," answered Yentsiao. "Pumei is waiting for me on the bank of the Panku River. It's because of her that I've wandered so far from home." Then the girls laughed and said, "Forget about your Pumei. All the most beautiful girls in the world have been brought here by the dragon. Now, where else could you find a better wife?"

Unable to refuse their offer Yentsiao looked at them hesitantly. He chanced to notice one girl who stood at some distance from him. She immediately hung her head. A sudden feeling of familiarity made Yentsiao say, "Very well, then I'll take that girl for my wife."

The girls wrapped the pearl in a dough made of wheat flour. Then they moulded this into the shape of a horse. They pulled a few hairs from the mane of Yentsiao's horse and stuck them on to the dough, and as the wind blew upon it, little by little the dough turned into a live horse of immense size. This they gave to the girl as the most valuable of gifts. After saying farewell, Yentsiao and the girl galloped off along the highroad.

As they rode along they came to a place where luxuriant bunches of red berries grew. "Tell me,"

Yentsiao asked, "are you the girl who fetched water from the Kuerpin River?"

His companion laughed and answered, "There are many girls in this world who look alike. But I am not that girl." Then Yentsiao said: "I don't think you are, for that girl always wore a red poppy in her hair." They talked as they rode until they came to a vast open space in the forest. Laughingly the girl asked, "What do you think of me?" After looking at her for a moment he answered: "Hm! You're very pretty."

"You really are foolish," the girl replied. "Why do you insist on chasing after Pumei, a girl you've never even seen yet?" Yentsiao answered: "Don't blame me. I must finish what I have started." "Oh I don't mind," she said. "If you like we can live together as sister and brother. Do you agree?" Yentsiao answered: "Yes. You're very kind, and when I have found your sister-in-law, I'll help you to find a suitable husband." She replied: "I thank you, but I'm afraid that when you find happiness you'll forget all about me."

Beyond the forest they came to a roaring river. On the opposite bank a log jutting out from a cave extended some way across the river. Remaining on their horses they urged them to swim across. When the horses neared the mouth of the cave after cross-

99

ing the river, they faltered and reared, and refused to go forward.

Yentsiao dismounted and looked into the mouth of the cave. Inside lay eight drunken demons, their heads resting on the log which jutted out over the river. At the mouth of the cave there was a poor, thin woman with a cangue around her neck. Her face was covered, but Yentsiao could hear her crying. Hearing Yentsiao approach she uncovered her face and looked up, then asked, "Why do you stop here? These eight demons eat human flesh. The instant they smell fresh human blood they wake up. They'll pounce on you like mad things. . . . Look, can you see that pile of human bones at the back of the cave? It's nearly as high as a tall pine tree."

"Who are you?" asked Yentsiao. "Why are you kept here?" Panting and sobbing, the woman answered, "My name is Nomingchiao. One day as I was picking up clams on the bank of the river the demons caught me. They brought me here and forced me to boil human meat for them. If I had refused they would have boiled me." Yentsiao was filled with rage. He said to the girl, "Sister, we can't pass by and do nothing to help this woman!"

At that moment, the leader of the demons, who was sleeping nearest to the mouth of the cave, stirred a little. Nomingchiao quickly pushed Yentsiao into the mouth of the cave and whispered, "Hurry, go to the back of the cave and dig up their magic axe, then you will be able to kill them." No sooner had Yentsiao run into the cave than he heard a demon shout, "I smell a stranger! What's going on?" Nomingchiao pointed to the girl on the horse and quickly answered: "Oh this is my younger sister. She has come a long way to bring you a gift. Here, do you like this pouch?"

By this time Yentsiao had dug up the magic axe with great effort and, afraid to waste even one moment he rushed towards the mouth of the cave. Before he was discovered by the leader of the demons, he had already chopped the seven others into halves.

Suddenly Yentsiao heard Nomingchiao shout, "Look out!" But the warning came too late. The leader of the demons had stolen up behind Yentsiao, caught him by the throat and was trying to force the axe out of his hand. Yentsiao was in such great pain that he broke into a terrible sweat. The girl jumped from her horse, quickly snatched a red-hot poker from the fire and burned the demon's back with it. This made the demon scream with pain and he released his hold of Yentsiao. Yentsiao swung round and sliced the demon in half. Then he freed Nomingchiao from the cangue.

To express her gratitude Nomingchiao gave Yentsiao a pouch which she had filled with a fragrant perfume. His Little Sister said, "Brother, you ride my magic horse. I'll ride with Nomingchiao on your horse and see that she reach her home safely."

"That's fine," agreed Yentsiao. "The Panku River isn't far from here. Follow in my tracks and we'll soon be there."

As Yentsiao's horse climbed a high ridge a cluster of dark clouds gathered in the sky completely hiding the sun. And although it was only midday it was as dark as night. The storm broke. The magic pearl horse, which Yentsiao was now riding, was beaten down by the wind and rain. It began to dwindle away until there was nothing left but the pearl. Meanwhile Yentsiao had taken shelter under a tree and was waiting for his Little Sister to catch up with him. He waited a long time but she did not come. Eventually Yentsiao scrambled down the ridge, landing in a swamp at the bottom. His feet sank into the mud. The air was thick with myriads of mosquitoes. Even the strongest of hunting horses would have been bitten to death by them.

Yentsiao took three steps forward and went into the mud right up to his waist. Another step and the mud was up to his chest. He wanted to shout for help but had not the strength to do so. Mosquitoes as large as birds flew into his face, their poisonous stings, piercing his skin. As Yentsiao stared at the giant mosquitoes hovering around him he noticed that none attempted to sting him on the chest, where the pouch hung. So he quickly opened the pouch and sprinkled some of the perfume over himself. The mosquitoes then flew away. All night long he could hear them buzzing, but they disappeared the next morning.

The sun was high in the sky when Yentsiao heard the sound of horse hoofs on the ridge above him. "There you are!" laughingly called his Little Sister. "I've been looking for you everywhere and you were right here all the time, taking a bath! Are you cooled off now!"

Yentsiao answered: "Don't make fun of me. Only pigs like to bathe in mud!"

"Why did you go so far ahead?" asked his Little Sister. "Wouldn't it have been better to stay on the ridge?" Yentsiao was annoyed by this remark and replied: "The Panku River is not on the ridge, is it? Perhaps you would have sunk deeper if you were me."

"Dear brother, if I were Pumei I'd love you all my life for your constancy, and still that wouldn't be enough. Let us go. Perhaps Pumei is already tired of waiting for you!"

They mounted the big horse together and were soon on the other side of the ninety-nine *li* swamp. As they descended a hill they saw smoke rising from the huts of the people who lived on the bank of the Panku River.

103

"We have reached the end of our journey," shouted Little Sister happily. "Go quickly. I'll wait here for you." Yentsiao thanked her for her help, then with a fast beating heart, he rode off. . . .

Everyone knew that Pumei's father, Yierchia, was not an easy man to deal with. So when Yentsiao came face to face with the old man he was on his guard. Yierchia looked critically at this young man, who had come from afar. Then he said: "Young man, many other young men have come to me for my daughter's hand in marriage and failed to win her. If you are determined to be a suitor I'll give you a test to see whether you are a suitable match for my daughter." Yentsiao answered: "Perhaps I'm not good enough for her but please let me see her. I wouldn't like to come here and then depart without seeing her!" Yierchia answered: "Don't be impatient. You shall see her but first you must do three things. Come with me."

A fast brown horse with a copper coin tied to its saddle was waiting outside. The old man struck the horse a fierce blow with his whip and it galloped off. After it had gone some distance the old man turned to Yentsiao and said, "Ride after him and shoot an arrow through the hole in the copper coin." Yentsiao patted his horse, flung himself over its back and into the saddle. Seconds later, Yentsiao's arrow whizzed

through the air towards the saddle on the back of the brown horse.

Soon afterwards, the brown horse returned to Yierchia with an arrow stuck in the hole of the coin. Pulling the arrow out Yierchia admitted, "You're a good marksman. But it's late now. Please go and rest for the night in the log hut over there."

No sooner had Yentsiao stepped through the door, than the old man locked him in and shouted, "Young man, if you find that you can't stay in there, call me. I have no wish to harm you."

As the room was pitch dark Yentsiao took out his dragon pearl and flashed it around. Then he saw that the room was full of giant mosquitoes and hornets. They swarmed round him like hungry demons. Hastily opening his pouch, he sprinkled the fragrant perfume over his body, and then lay down to sleep.

Long after daybreak Yierchia put his ear to the door and listened but could not hear anything. So he quickly opened the door and saw the young man sleeping peacefully. As Yentsiao yawned and began to stretch, Yierchia noticed there was sweat on his brow. All around him the floor was black with mosquitoes and hornets starved to death. With a laugh Yentsiao sat up and said, "Thank you for the use of your guest room, it was much better than sleeping in a tent." "Don't mention it," replied

Yierchia, somewhat embarrassed. "Now I'm going to see if your love for my daughter is really sincere."

When Yentsiao stepped outside the hut he saw a girl wearing a red poppy in her hair. She was tied to a stake on a platform! Flames licked around her. They were so fierce and the heat was so great that the people, who had gathered to watch were forced to stand at a distance. In a clear voice she sang:

> *Oh hunter of the Kuerpin River,*
> *Yentsiao my courageous lover.*
> *You've suffered many hardships,*
> *And all of them for me, dear boy.*
> *Come my love, now is the hour,*
> *We can unite as one!*
> *In my heart there is only joy!*

Yentsiao looked intently and saw that she was the girl, who used to fetch water from the Kuerpin River and her features were exactly those of the Little Sister whom he had rescued from the dragon. He was completely puzzled by this. "Who are you? Hurry! Please tell me!" shouted Yentsiao. Throwing the red poppy to him she said, "Yentsiao, I am Pumei and Pumei is me! I'm the girl you're looking for! Don't you understand?" Taking the magic axe from his saddle and holding it high, Yentsiao dashed towards the wall of flames. He hacked down the flaming platform. The girl leaped into his arms. The glowing fire lit up their smiling faces. Yentsiao carried Pumei to the big horse and lifted her on to its back. "Stay a moment, I must say goodbye to my father first," pleaded Pumei. Looking at his son-in-law Yierchia knew that he would never find his like again in this world. Turning to his daughter he asked, "What would you like me to give you for your dowry? You can have anything that is within my power to grant."

"I already have something ready," answered Pumei, and from the house she fetched two birch-bark buckets, each pierced by an arrow. As Yentsiao took them from her he asked, "Pumei, you say you love me but why did you make me suffer so?"

"Yentsiao, I had to make sure what kind of a man you were before I could marry you, don't you agree?" Pumei answered.

"Of course, I understand now. You're a clever girl." The big horse neighed, and tossed its great head. It was time for Yentsiao to depart for home with his wife.

Kumiya

(A Pulang Story)

It is said that in far off times, heaven and earth did not exist; there were neither plants nor people; only dark clouds floating everywhere. The great magician, a giant named Kumiya and his twelve sons made up their minds to create a world and put many things in it. Without wasting a moment they began to look for materials with which to build this world.

In those times there was a rhinoceros, who was a friend and companion of the clouds. He roamed together with the clouds through the vast spaces of the universe.

When Kumiya discovered the rhinoceros he stripped him of his hide and used that to make the sky. Then he gathered together the beautiful clouds to make a suit of clothes for the sky. The eyes of the rhinoceros he made into stars and cast them out into the sky to twinkle. The earth he made from the flesh of the animal; rocks from its bones; water from its blood; and from its hair many kinds of trees, bushes, grass and flowers. Lastly, he took the brains of the rhinoceros and made out of them a man and a woman. From the marrow of its bones he fashioned all kinds of birds, beasts, reptiles and fish.

Kumiya suspended the sky in space; but he had no way of propping it up and was afraid it might fall! Below it hung the earth which, too, had nothing to hold it up. Afraid it might suddenly turn over, clever Kumiya soon thought out a way to solve the problem. He changed the legs of the rhinoceros into four pillars and placed one under each corner of the sky, at the north, south, east and west, to hold it up. Kumiya then caught a huge sea-turtle to support the earth upon its back. The sea-turtle was unwilling to do this and was always thinking of running away. As even a slight movement of the turtle shook the whole earth, Kumiya chose his most loyal golden cock to guard the turtle and ensure that it did not run away. If the sea-turtle moved the cock pecked at its eyes. But sometimes when the cock grew tired and dozed off the sea-turtle would move a little and then there were great earthquakes. Even now when the earth trembles people quickly sprinkle rice on the ground so that the golden cock will wake up to eat the grain, and so remain on guard.

In this way the sky was held up and earth made firm. Beautiful clouds floated across the sky and the brilliant stars twinkled brightly. On the earth below, the people went about their daily life. Birds darted here and there and they flew through the air; bees sipped nectar from the abundant clusters of flowers; deer roamed over the hill tops; and fish frolicked in the streams and lakes.

Kumiya and his sons smiled, for their world was spacious and beautiful!

Then came misfortune! The nine sun sisters and the nine moon brothers who were on bad terms with Kumiya became jealous of his success. They wanted to destroy the beautiful world he had created. Combining their strength, they shot devastating rays of heat at the earth in an effort to destroy it.

The beautiful clouds faded away and the brilliant stars lost their lustre. The dry earth cracked; the crops died from lack of moisture; the flowers, the grass and the trees all withered away. Even the rocks melted. And to this very day many footprints, resembling those made by men and cattle can be seen on the big rock at Silver Hill, in Chinping County. The heat of the suns was so fierce that it burned off the crabs' heads, snakes' feet and frogs' tails. It also burned out the fish's tongues. That is why today a crab has no head, a snake no feet, a frog no tail and a fish no tongue.

It was so hot that, when he went out, Kumiya had to wax his bamboo rain-hat to protect himself from the heat. But the sun melted the wax, and it rolled down into his eyes and scalded them. Angrily Kumiya vowed, "If I don't destroy you suns and moons, I'm not the Kumiya that created heaven and earth!" He strode into the forest, felled a tree and made a bow. Then he looked about until he found a vine strong enough to make a bow-string and a bamboo stout enough for arrows. He dipped the tips of the arrows in the poisonous water of the Dragon Lake. The making of his bow and arrows completed, Kumiya walked across rocks as hot as burning coals and swam across rivers as hot as boiling water. The sweat poured off his body like rain. He overcame many obstacles and finally reached the top of the highest mountain peak.

The nine sun sisters and the nine moon brothers were now so elated that they began to show off. They hurled down still more heat and burning sparks to scorch the earth. Filled with hatred and indignation, from the top of the peak, Kumiya stood and watched. Ignoring the sweat and scarcely taking time to draw breath he fitted an arrow to his bow, aimed it and hit one of the suns. A noise like thunder shook the earth. The sun, spitting fire, rolled to the foot of the mountain. The remaining eight suns and nine moons flew into a rage. Determined to burn up the earth completely they joined together to attack Kumiya, intending to scorch him to death first. But arrow after arrow darted through the sky and one by one Kumiya killed the suns and moons. Blood from the wounded suns and moons poured down from the sky like rain. Then the earth cooled down. The withered crops, the grass and the trees came to life again and once more the flowers blossomed. Blood of the suns and moons fell on the earth, on the leaves of trees, on flowers and on the feet of white pheasants. It stained all of them red.

At last only one sun and one moon were left in the sky. When they saw their sisters and brothers killed they were afraid and began to hasten across the sky.

Kumiya was now very tired and not much strength was left in his arms, but his anger had not cooled. With difficulty he fixed the seventeenth arrow to his bow and shot at the last moon. Because of his weakness and the swift flight of the moon, he missed. But though he missed, the arrow passed so close to the moon that it became cold with fear. It became so cold that it froze, and it has never become warm again. Thus one sun and one moon escaped and they were so afraid of Kumiya's arrows that they went far away and did not dare to show their faces again.

Without a moon and a sun the earth became cold and dark. Time was no longer divided into day and night, rivers ceased to flow and the leaves no longer trembled in the breeze. The people had to put lanterns on the horns of their oxen, when they

ploughed their fields, and use golden bamboo canes when they went out to prevent stumbling. How could they survive these cold, dark days?

Kumiya decided that he should seek out the sun and moon and ask them to come back and give light and warmth again to the earth. So he sent a swallow to find out where they were hiding.

Several days later the swallow returned and reported to Kumiya, "The sun and moon are hiding in a cave at the eastern end of the sky."

Then Kumiya called a meeting of all the beasts and fowls to discuss things with them. He proposed to invite the sun and moon to come back. They all agreed with him and said they were willing to suffer the hardships of the long journey to the east to invite the sun and moon to return.

The white-headed and black-headed partridges were the only creatures who were unwilling to go. The black-headed partridge dyed his tail red and said: "I'm ill. Look at my tail! I can't even fly, my feathers are stained with blood. I cannot go!" The other partridge bleached his head white and said: "My mother and father have just died. See, I'm still wearing a mourning band for them. I cannot leave home at this time!" From that day on the white head of one kind of partridge and the red tail of another became symbols of selfishness, laziness and cowardice. They were laughed at and scorned by everyone.

The creatures who were going to invite the sun and moon to return set out on their errand in high spirits. The swallows led the procession. They were followed by the fireflies who lit the way. Because the rooster was the best at making his voice heard he took command of all the creatures that flew. The wild boar who was the strongest and most daring animal was in charge of all the creatures that walked. Kumiya stayed behind because the sun and moon were afraid of him.

The sun and moon had become husband and wife while hiding in the cave. But they worried by day and by night, for they knew that if they hid too long in the cave, they would die from starvation and lack of fresh air. They wanted to return to the beautiful earth but they were afraid that Kumiya would shoot with his arrows and kill them. They embraced each other and wept. Just at the very moment, when their fear was greatest, they heard a loud clamour outside the cave. They became even more terrified and huddled in a corner of the cave, hardly daring to breathe lest they betray their presence.

The procession of creatures arrived at the mouth of the cave. They began to shout, calling on the sun and moon to come out. But not one sound came from within the cave. The rooster asked all the creatures to be quiet and as soon as there was silence he ruffled his beautiful feathers, stretched out his neck and with a long cock-a-doodle-doo called out:

> Oh brilliant sun, please turn about.
> Moon of the night, come quickly out.
> Come quickly, come quickly for
> Heat and light we cannot do without!

The rooster was so earnest, yet so courteous, and his voice was so friendly and encouraging that the sun and moon lost some of their fear and replied:

> Here without air and food we'd rather stay,
> Lest Kumiya's arrows pierce us through.
> Should we come, it will do no good.
> We'll starve, for no one will feed us.

The creatures all sang in chorus:

> Kumiya, it is, who asks you to return.
> You need not be afraid that you'll die.
> His daughter Shafeima will feed you everyday.
> She'll attend to her duty, come what may.

It was difficult for the sun and moon to believe that Kumiya had really forgiven them, and they were still afraid to leave the cave. Once again all the creatures tried to convince them but failed. Finally the rooster made a bargain with the sun and moon. He said: "From now on, you come out only when I crow and stay in when I am silent, thus there

115

will be no danger for you." To make them trust him the rooster cut a knot of wood into halves as a pledge. One half he threw into the cave and the other part he fixed on his own head. That is why today the rooster has a comb on his head; and why from that day onwards the task of awakening the sun at dawn has always been carried out by the rooster. If a rooster fails to do this he is usually killed by his master.

Every day Shafeima had to feed the sun and moon. At dawn she appeared as a beautiful girl, at noon as a healthy young woman and at night as a grey-haired old woman. Each day she fed the sun with molten gold and the moon with molten silver.

In obedience to the wish of Kumiya everybody requested the sun to come out by day and the moon at night. They were promised that they would be allowed to meet in the cave on the first and last day of each month. Because the sun was timid and afraid of darkness, so it was decided that she should come out during the day. As she was also shy, the moon gave her a packet of needles and told her to use them to blind the eyes of anyone who stared into her face when she was in the sky.

At last everything was agreed upon, and the sun and moon were willing to come out. But the entrance to the cave was blocked by a large rock. All the creatures pulled and tugged but could not move it.

Then the wild boar wiggled his big ears and said: "All right, everybody step aside and let me try." He gave the stone a big jolt and it rolled to one side.

The sun came out first and the moon followed, making day and night. Everywhere on earth it was bright and warm. When the sun shone on the crest of the hill all the animals began to rejoice. When it shone over the forest all the birds began to sing. When it shone, fish splashed and leaped with delight, old men mended their ploughs, old women took up their spinning, young men went to the fields to work, young girls went to the hills to gather firewood, and the boys took the cattle to the pasture. And when the moon's shimmering rays flooded the world with silver light the old men told their happy tales. When its rays lit up the ground the children gaily romped and shouted while young people played their flutes and strummed on their two-stringed lutes. . . .

Everyone was filled with joy and hope. The world became even more beautiful than before!

The Heavenly Flute Player

(A Li Story)

Long, long ago at the foot of Five-Finger Mountain there lived a man who played with great skill and beauty upon the bamboo flute. The music he made was more melodious than the song of the oriole; its trills were more clear than those of the thrush; and its rhapsody surpassed the song of the soaring lark. When he played his flute, the birds would pause in their flight and the peasants would rest from their work in the fields. At the sound of his music old men would smile and feel again the delight of youth while children would dance and jump with joy. Because of the charm of his music people thought he must be more than mortal and called him the Heavenly Flute Player.

One day the Dragon King of the South Sea gave a banquet to which he invited a great company of immortals. The king, dressed in his dragon gown and wearing a jade belt, sat feasting with his guests, all arrayed in strange and splendid garments. It happened that just at this time the Heavenly Flute Player reached the seashore, after walking for ten days and nights. Casting his fishing-net into the tranquil sea, he seated himself on a boulder and began to play on his bamboo flute. Just as the Dragon King raised his cup to toast the immortals, his ears caught the strains of this enchanting music. The guests were so enthralled by it that the jade cups slipped from between their fingers and fell to the ground, and they quite forgot the feast in front of them. The Heavenly Flute Player was not aware that immortals were listening to him while the immortals felt certain that the flute player was one of themselves and must have descended from heaven.

The Dragon King was so charmed with the delightful music, that he wished to invite the Player to teach his son. He traced the source of the music, until he found the man. The Heavenly Flute Player agreed to teach his son and, pulling in his net, thrust the bamboo flute into his belt and went off with the Dragon King to his palace.

Soon he became homesick. Time seemed slow and one day was for him like a year. At the end of three long years, the Dragon King's son had finally learned how to play the flute and the Heavenly Flute Player asked the king to let him go home. The Dragon King was pleased that his son had learned to play the flute and decided to reward the teacher with a handsome gift. He told his son to take his teacher to a treasure-house to select two treasures for himself.

The Heavenly Flute Player and his pupil entered the large store-house where all the Dragon King's treasures, numbering hundreds of thousands, were kept. On one shelf were precious stones of all colours — red, green, yellow, blue and violet. Weighing ten catties each they glittered with a dazzling brilliance. On another shelf gleamed heavy ingots of gold. Bamboo baskets of all sizes hung on the wall; and in a cupboard were reed rain-cloaks of different lengths.

The Heavenly Flute Player walked around, then stopped in front of the bamboo baskets. He mused, if I take one of these, I'll have something in which to carry the fish and shrimps I catch. So he took one of the medium-sized bamboo baskets from the wall and tied it to his belt.

Then he walked round again and stopped by a cupboard of rain-cloaks, thinking, if I take one of these, I will be able to go fishing even when it rains. With this in mind, he took a medium-sized reed rain-cloak out of the cupboard and threw it about his shoulders.

After he had made his choice, the Dragon King's son led him out of the treasure-house.

"Why do you prefer these ordinary things to the precious stones, gold and silver?" asked the boy.

"Gold and silver are not the most useful things," the Heavenly Flute Player replied with a smile. "After some time they will be spent. But now that I have this cloak and basket, I can go fishing every day and I'll never starve."

When he reached home, the Heavenly Flute Player found, to his great surprise, that the bamboo basket and the reed rain-cloak were not the ordinary articles he thought they were, but were real treasures. And from that time on whenever he returned home very hungry after a fishing trip, there was always delicious food, ready to eat, in his basket; and whenever he wished to go to the South Sea to catch fish or to the East Sea to net shrimps, the reed rain-cloak spread like a pair of wings and carried him there.

After many years, with the bamboo basket on his back and the reed rain-cloak round his shoulders, the Heavenly Flute Player flew up to the top of the Five-Finger Mountain and played on his flute, its enchanting tunes ringing in the clouds. Ever since then his music has brought joy and happiness to all the people.